The Look On Bryce Lexington's Handsome Face Said It All.

He liked what he saw, liked it very much. Paige felt an inexplicable tingle of excitement as he continued to stare at her. She quickly pulled the beach jacket on, covering her body from shoulders to midthigh.

"Tomorrow, Bradford..." Drew paused to take a calming breath. "Tomorrow bring your own swimsuit." He quickly turned and left the pool house without even pausing to look back.

Paige closed her eyes. The look of smoldering intensity that Drew had greeted her with popped back into her mind. A tremor of sensual desire made its way through her body, then settled low inside her.

Paige was not sure what she wanted anymore or why she was still there. She probably should have resigned as she had originally planned, but now it was too late.

Dear Reader,

Dog days of summer got you down? Chill out and relax with six brand-new love stories from Silhouette Desire!

August's MAN OF THE MONTH is the first book in the exciting family-based saga BECKETT'S FORTUNE by Dixie Browning. *Beckett's Cinderella* features a hero honor-bound to repay a generations-old debt and a poor-but-proud heroine leery of love and money she can't believe is offered unconditionally. *His E-Mail Order Wife* by Kristi Gold, in which matchmaking relatives use the Internet to find a high-powered exec a bride, is the latest title in the powerful DYNASTIES: THE CONNELLYS series.

A daughter seeking revenge discovers love instead in *Falling for the Enemy* by Shawna Delacorte. Then, in *Millionaire Cop & Mom-To-Be* by Charlotte Hughes, a jilted, pregnant bride is rescued by her childhood sweetheart.

Passion flares between a family-minded rancher and a marriage-shy divorcée in Kathie DeNosky's *Cowboy Boss*. And a pretend marriage leads to undeniable passion in *Desperado Dad* by Linda Conrad.

So find some shade, grab a cold one…and read all six passionate, powerful and provocative new love stories from Silhouette Desire this month.

Enjoy!

Joan Marlow Golan

Joan Marlow Golan
Senior Editor, Silhouette Desire

Please address questions and book requests to:
Silhouette Reader Service
U.S.: 3010 Walden Ave., P.O. Box 1325, Buffalo, NY 14269
Canadian: P.O. Box 609, Fort Erie, Ont. L2A 5X3

Falling for
the Enemy
SHAWNA DELACORTE

Silhouette
Desire

Published by Silhouette Books
America's Publisher of Contemporary Romance

SILHOUETTE BOOKS

ISBN 0-373-76455-3

FALLING FOR THE ENEMY

Visit Silhouette at www.eHarlequin.com

Printed in U.S.A.

SHAWNA DELACORTE

has delayed her move to Washington State, staying in the Midwest in order to spend some additional time with family. She still travels as often as time permits and is looking forward to visiting several new places during the upcoming year while continuing to devote herself to writing full-time. Shawna would appreciate hearing from her readers. She can be reached at 6505 E. Central, Box #300, Wichita, KS 67206-1924.

One

"**P**aige Bradford? I'm Bryce Lexington." Bryce rose from his chair and held out his hand as she entered his office.

Even though he had seen her photograph in her personnel file, this incredibly beautiful woman was not what he had anticipated. Her firm handshake showed confidence. She appeared composed and at ease. Everything about her was a surprise and he instantly liked everything he saw. An unexpected tightness constricted his chest when their hands touched. He took a deep breath in an attempt to break the sensation. This unmistakable physical attraction toward her was both ill-timed and unacceptable considering the circumstances.

According to Joe Thompkins, his corporate head of security, Paige had been surreptitiously prying into Bryce's personal life for the past six months and two weeks ago had procured a job at his corporate headquarters in Santa Monica, California. Now she stood in his office on the other side of his desk looking as desirable as any woman he had ever met. What was her game? What was she after? Again, a quick rush of excitement darted through his body. He shoved it away and focused on the business at hand. He indicated a chair for her, then sat down behind his desk.

Paige settled into the chair he had indicated. "It's a pleasure to meet you, Mr. Lexington."

She had seen hundreds of pictures of him and read every word she could find that had been written about him—magazines, newspapers and even the Internet. None of it had prepared her for a face-to-face meeting with this dynamic man. Paige had accepted his handshake, then quickly withdrawn her hand from his grasp. An intimate warmth had traveled up her arm and spread through her body, leaving her momentarily unsure about her chosen course of action.

She clenched her jaw and rallied her determination. She would not allow his good looks and some errant twinge of unwanted desire to divert her from the all-important task she had set for herself. She would see to it that Bryce Lexington was held accountable for his actions. That the world would know he was nothing more than an unprincipled shark who was responsible for her father's suicide.

"Your personnel file shows that you possess the educational background, skill level and computer experience necessary for the position as my administrative assistant. Our corporate policy is to promote from within whenever possible. Since you agreed to come in for the interview, I'll take that to mean you're interested in the position."

"Yes, Mr. Lexington. I feel that—"

"Call me Bryce."

"All right...*Bryce*. I'm extremely interested in the position and would consider it an honor to work as your administrative assistant. I have long admired your dedication to charity and your hard work in that regard.'' She smiled, doing her best to project as much sincerity as she could muster and thankful that she hadn't choked on the audacious lies.

"Do you have a current passport?''

"Yes.''

Without warning, he rose from his chair and moved to the office door. "That's it, Bradford.''

His abrupt action startled her. "That's what?''

"End of the interview. The job is yours effective immediately.'' He glanced at his watch. "You have three hours to pack. We're going to London and we'll be gone for five days. Meet me at the company hangar at the airport. Get the directions from Eileen.'' He opened the door and stepped aside, indicating that she was dismissed.

"I…uh, I appreciate this opportunity—''

"I have another meeting, Bradford. Eileen will provide you with what you need.''

"Yes…thank you.'' She hurried out of the office, a little uncertain about exactly what had just happened. The office door closed behind her. She was momentarily irritated with his brusque manner, which had almost bordered on rude.

"Amazing, isn't he?''

A female voice cut into Paige's thoughts. She turned toward the sound, then glanced at the closed office door once more before giving her full attention to the woman approaching her. "I have to admit that was the oddest interview I've ever had…and certainly the shortest.''

The woman extended her hand and a warm smile. "We haven't met officially. I'm Eileen Draper, the office manager.''

Eileen handed Paige a sheet of paper containing the information about the location of the company jet. It also contained all pertinent names, addresses, phone numbers and fax numbers of key personnel. Paige noted in amazement that her name had already been added to the list.

"You'll be staying at the corporate flat in London. The address and phone number are listed." Eileen glanced toward Bryce's closed office door, then lowered her voice. "In case you haven't guessed, he's a true workaholic in every sense of the word, but he doesn't expect any more from others than he's willing to give himself. Right now he's in the middle of several very big deals, so things are more hectic than usual. Just keep calm and try not to let him muddle your head with too many things at once. And most importantly, don't be afraid to stand up to him if he starts driving you crazy. Underneath he's really a very caring and considerate man, straightforward and honest."

Eileen offered Paige a confident smile. "I'm sure you'll do just fine."

Paige headed for the elevator, her thoughts not as positive as Eileen's words had been. *Straightforward and honest...hmmph! That'll be the day.* She took the elevator to the first floor and exited the building. She paused on the sidewalk and glanced up toward the third-floor window of Bryce's office. *Pretty soon everyone will know the real truth about you, Bryce Lexington, and your underhanded business tactics.* She continued toward her car.

Bryce watched from his office window as Paige walked down the sidewalk. As soon as she was out of sight he picked up the phone and called Joe Thompkins. A minute later his security chief arrived in his office. Bryce settled into his chair, leaned back and propped his feet up on his desk. He listened intently as the forty-two-year-old ruggedly handsome man opened a file folder and gave him a quick rundown.

"Paige Bradford, maiden name Franklin. Thirty-two

years old. Daughter of Stanley Franklin, founder of Franklin Industries. Mother deceased. Following a divorce one year ago from Jerry Bradford, Paige moved from St. Louis back to her father's house in Los Angeles. She's the one who discovered his body after he shot himself. That was six months ago. It was shortly after that when she began tracking down information about you.''

Bryce took the folder from Joe and looked over the contents as he slowly shook his head. ''If she hadn't tried to pass herself off as a writer doing an in-depth biography of me, then called one of my business associates, Herb Fenwick, to set up an interview with him we probably wouldn't have known about her activities. Fortunately, Herb called me after she'd contacted him.''

Bryce scanned the folder again. ''I'm not sure what type of person I was expecting, but she certainly wasn't it. I wonder what she wants with me. It can't have anything to do with my purchase of Franklin Industries. Surely she knows about her father, what he did and why the deal went down that way.''

''The real kicker was her procuring a job right here in corporate headquarters with access to your entire computer network. You have a copy of her personnel record, don't you?''

''Yes.'' Bryce reached in a desk drawer and withdrew another file folder. He looked through the pages, his gaze lingering for a moment longer than necessary on the photograph that did not do her justice. It did not show her beautiful smile or her sparkling hazel eyes. He let out a sigh of exasperation. ''I suppose the sensible thing to do would have been to just ask her what she was up to. There could be a perfectly logical reason for her running around prying into my life and business.''

''Oh, really?'' Joe's expression and tone of voice said

he found Bryce's suggestion totally ludicrous. "And just what do you suppose that *perfectly logical* reason might be?"

Bryce shot him an exasperated look. "All right, let's say she does have some sort of ulterior motive for her actions. We don't want to make any accusations without some type of proof." Bryce suddenly sat up straighter, his tone of voice taking on a sense of urgency. "She hasn't done anything detrimental to the company, like compromising sensitive corporate information, has she?"

"Not that I'm aware of. Her investigations seem to have been limited to publicly available information...so far."

Bryce studied her file a moment longer, then closed it with a finality that said the discussion was finished. "I've transferred her to my personal staff as my administrative assistant effective today. According to her file she's fully qualified for the job. That way I can keep my eye on her until we figure out what she's up to—*if* she's up to anything at all—and she won't know we're suspicious of her. I don't want to tip our hand and frighten her off before we find out what this is about."

"I don't like it, Bryce. She seems to have some sort of personal agenda she's pursuing and you can bet it's *not* to your benefit."

Bryce opened the file and stared at her photograph again. "You know—" he flashed a grin "—it's worth a little bit of inconvenience to have someone around who looks like this. Eileen Draper is a dear and I couldn't get along without her management skills, but she is old enough to be my mother." He stole a guilty look toward the office door, then turned a sheepish expression to Joe. "And don't you dare tell Eileen I said that."

Bryce closed the folder and tossed it onto the corner of his desk, his manner once again turning to serious business.

"I'll play it by ear, take it one day at a time. We'll see where things progress from here."

"You want her working directly with you where she would be free to pursue whatever she has on her agenda up to and including doing you physical harm?"

"In all fairness, Joe, we don't know that she has anything in mind that's damaging to me or to the corporation."

"That's your final decision in the matter?"

"Yep. That's the way I intend to play it."

"I want to go on record as being dead set against this, Bryce."

"Your objection is duly noted."

Joe returned to his duties, leaving Bryce at his desk. Bryce's thoughts returned to his brief encounter with Paige. He was pleased that she did not seem afraid of him. He knew his position and manner were often intimidating to others, but he was a busy man and didn't have the time or desire to deal with unnecessary pleasantness. More than once he'd been told his handling of the social graces was occasionally less than adequate. He knew how to play the game when he needed to, but he felt that all the pretenses were a waste of time and definitely not his style.

He thoroughly disliked the little mind games of one-upmanship and psychological power control, both in business and in his personal life. He didn't understand why people couldn't be honest with each other. It would certainly save a lot of time and make life much easier.

A stab of guilt provided him with a sharp reminder of the blatant dishonesty and subterfuge he had perpetrated not half an hour ago in his office. He was not pleased about it, but the circumstances were unique. The necessity created by the situation overruled his displeasure and eased his pangs of conscience.

Bryce found all the little dating games and rituals a waste

of time, too. He suspected it was one of the reasons it was so difficult for him to develop a personal and lasting relationship with a woman. An errant thought crept into his reality as he wondered if he would ever be able to find the right woman.

It was not as if he was asking for the moon. All he wanted was an intelligent woman with a sense of humor who also possessed a healthy dose of solid common sense and was able to stand on her own two feet. Someone who was gentle and compassionate, but could be tough when the situation called for it. Someone well-read, with an appreciation of the arts, who also liked outdoor activities. Someone honest and forthright whom he could trust and with whom he could share. Someone he could give his heart and his love to.

No, he wasn't asking for the moon—just the entire solar system and all the stars beyond. He knew his requirements were impossibly high. With each passing year he came closer to the sad realization that his chances of finding someone he could love without reservation were growing more and more remote. Eileen had told him on more than one occasion that he worked too hard and had closed off his life to everything but his business interests. Bryce didn't want to believe her, but he knew deep down inside that she might be right. What he did not know was what he could do about it.

Was this the one thing that the man who had been dubbed *the master of the golden touch* would find too elusive? His business holdings, no matter how lucrative, could not keep him warm at night. They could not help him celebrate his successes or grapple with sorrow at sad occasions. They could not share his dreams. They were only material possessions, nothing more.

Bryce tried to sort out his impressions of Paige Bradford—she had definitely made an indelible impression on him. She wore her auburn hair swept up on her head. Her hazel eyes sparkled with intelligence and confidence. He recalled the way her hand felt in his, the subtle fragrance of her perfume, the tailored lines of her clothes and the way they fit her body. He frowned as another image presented itself—the way she stared at him, as if trying to get inside his head and read what was going on there.

He rose from his chair and headed toward the office door. A twinge of uncertainty pricked at his consciousness. Maybe Joe had been right. Perhaps hiring Paige Bradford had been a really bad idea.

Paige stared at the clothes hanging in her closet as the time grew closer and closer to the moment of departure. She didn't have a clue about what to pack for five days in London, or what type of situations she would be encountering. She didn't want to look foolish by overpacking, but didn't want to be caught unprepared either.

She shook her head as she frowned. Even though she thought she'd studied Bryce Lexington so thoroughly that she knew him inside out, she had been totally unprepared for the man who had greeted her when she walked into his office. The photographs she had seen of him depicted a handsome man, but she could now say with complete confidence that the camera did not do him justice. His dark hair was thick and tended toward the longish side. He had a deep golden tan. And those eyes—they weren't blue, they were the most incredibly brilliant turquoise.

She had also been surprised by the way he was dressed. As the head of a corporate conglomerate with international holdings, she had just assumed Bryce would wear a suit to the office, especially to conduct a job interview. Instead, he wore jeans, a pullover shirt and running shoes. The shirt accentuated his broad shoulders and strong arms without the effect seeming to have been his intention.

And it was not just his physical appearance that had captured her undivided attention, either. His commanding presence had filled the large office. It was an intoxicating combination of power, wealth and confidence, yet did not present itself in the form of an inflated ego or arrogance in spite of his somewhat brusque manner. *At least not yet,* she cynically reminded herself. She knew a man like Bryce Lexington would soon show his true colors, and when he did she would be there to capitalize on it.

Paige dismissed any further speculation. She finally packed one suitcase, her decisions dictated more by the necessities of the tight time frame he had given her rather than practical considerations.

She barely had time after packing to stop at the post office to make arrangements to have her mail held. She didn't dare be late meeting her new boss at the airport. She knew a man like Bryce Lexington would not tolerate being kept waiting. It would not be a good start to their relationship and would hinder the next phase of her quest, searching for the information she needed to exact her revenge and expose him to the world.

Paige snorted in disgust. The word *relationship* usually pertained to something positive, to something good. But not in this case, not when the relationship in question was between herself and Bryce Lexington. She mentally steeled herself against the difficulties she would need to endure along the path she had chosen. She turned the corner and pulled her car into the parking lot at the company hangar.

Bryce was waiting for her and hurried her onto the private jet. Precisely on schedule, as was everything that surrounded Bryce Lexington, they lifted off into the evening sky. To her surprise, as soon as they were airborne he went to the small galley, opened a bottle of wine and poured two glasses. She had assumed he would have hired someone to handle these chores.

"Here, Bradford." He set the glasses on opposite sides of a table. "We'll have something to eat then get right to work."

"We'll be working during the flight?" She heard a hint of irritation in her voice, but hadn't been able to stop it. That possibility had not occurred to her. It had already been a long, full day.

He cocked his head and stared at her. "Do you have a problem with that?"

She quickly regained her composure. "No…of course not. This just seems like an odd place to try to get some work done, not really a business setting." She tried to offer a smile that said she was not upset by his long workday, but she wasn't sure how successful she had been.

"I do very little work at the Santa Monica corporate offices. I doubt I'm there more than two or three days a month. I prefer to work in more comfortable surroundings. I maintain a full office at my home, where I usually work when I'm in town."

Bryce toyed with his wineglass, running his fingertip around the rim, then turning the stem between his fingers. It was not so much a nervous habit as an effort to focus his attention on the business aspects of what was happening and away from his very personal thoughts about the attractive woman sitting across from him.

His nostrils flared slightly as he inhaled the same tantalizing fragrance that she'd worn at the interview. He seldom made mistakes, but this time he had made a big one. He definitely should have listened to Joe and not brought her into his office, but not for the reasons Joe had presented. Bryce's reasons were far more personal and definitely involved his libido. He took another sip of wine. "I can't think of any reason to waste all the time it takes to fly to London when we could be accomplishing something worthwhile."

Accomplishing something worthwhile. Paige turned his words over in her mind. Was his definition of worthwhile based on how much money it made him? "What do you believe makes an accomplishment worthwhile? Is it based on ethical considerations or monetary results? What criteria do you use for judging it?"

He leveled a serious gaze at her. "That sounds like a loaded question. Why don't you tell me what's really on your mind?"

An uncomfortable shiver moved through Paige's body. Bryce seemed to be reading her mind. She should never have said anything about ethics. The words had just sort of slipped out before she could stop them. She took a deep breath and slowly expelled it before responding, but it didn't stop the nervous tingle.

"I didn't have anything particular on my mind," she said. "I guess I must have worded my question badly. I was only wondering if you were talking about your business activities or your charitable concerns."

"Why do you think there would be any difference in the way the two areas are handled?" he asked. "Ethics apply to both circumstances, and monetary results are simply a way of measuring business success, but it's not the be-all and end-all of everything. I like to think that I treat all situations with the same consideration, the same rules applying regardless of the type of project."

"I'm sorry...I didn't mean to imply that—"

"Forget it, Bradford." He clipped his words. "No harm done." Bryce rose from his chair and took two dinner trays from the refrigerator and put them into the microwave.

When Paige had gotten up this morning from a good

night's sleep, she'd had no idea that she would be on her way to London in a private jet before the day was through with the very man who had been the focus of all her energy for the past six months—the man she had sworn would pay for what he had done to her father.

She sipped her wine while she watched Bryce locate the silverware and napkins and some place mats for the table. He seemed to be pure nonstop energy. Paige couldn't imagine how many things must be going around inside his mind at one time. She considered that maybe she could just ask him about what happened between him and her father, but immediately dismissed it as being a totally unacceptable idea. There was no way that she trusted him to be honest with her in spite of his little speech about handling all things in an ethical manner. Maybe that speech fooled some people, but not her.

She knew if she even alluded to who she was, it would put him on his guard, then she would never be able to dig out the truth. He might even end up destroying some of the evidence she needed. She had maneuvered herself into an excellent position to find out what had really happened. It was better to simply continue with the plan that was already in place.

The image of her father slumped over his desk with the gun still in his hand had been burned into her memory. He had left a hand-written note that said:

I'm sorry, Paige. There was no other way. Please forgive my weakness.

She had found a partially destroyed file folder smoldering in the fireplace. What remained of the file made no more sense to her than her father's suicide note, but she had saved it anyway. She was shocked to find that her father's company was in such deep financial trouble. That he had long ago cashed in his life insurance. That even his house was mortgaged to the hilt. She sold the house and what little money that remained was barely enough to pay for his funeral.

Everything would have been all right if Bryce Lexington hadn't suddenly cut off negotiations with her father for the purchase of Franklin Industries. The worst part, and the thing that had aroused her suspicions, was that he managed to gain control of her father's company anyway and at a fraction of the original price—literally pennies on the dollar. What would happen to the people who depended on Franklin Industries to support their families? Would he throw them out like yesterday's newspaper? The fate of her father's employees was a situation that bothered her a great deal. So far the company was still in operation, but for how long? Somehow she had to find a way to ensure that their jobs were protected, but she didn't have a clue how...yet.

Since then Paige had made finding out everything about Bryce Lexington her number-one priority. He was thirty-eight years old and stood six-one. He possessed a genius IQ, graduating from high school at the age of fifteen. By the time he turned twenty-one he had earned a bachelor's degree in history, a second bachelor's degree in fine art and a master's degree in business administration. Certainly an unusual combination of educational interests and pursuits. He spoke fluent French, German, Italian and Spanish. What she had not found was any record of him ever being married, something she thought very odd.

Bryce seemed to have fooled everyone into believing he was quite a remarkable man, but she knew better. One way or another she intended to get the proof she needed and prove his responsibility in her father's suicide.

Paige slowly shook her head from side to side. In spite

of all the information she had gathered about him, he was not what she had expected. She caught herself just in time. For a moment she had been about to admit that she was impressed, that there was a little bit of admiration on her part, but that would never do. She needed to keep herself focused on her true purpose. She had to find proof that his unethical business practices were responsible for ruining her father and do what she could to protect the jobs of his employees. She took another sip of wine as her gaze wandered back to Bryce.

The intensity of his eyes and the concentrated energy of his stare startled her. Her swallow of wine went down the wrong way, causing a choking cough.

He took the wineglass from her hand and set it on the table, a look of genuine concern crossing his face. "Are you all right?"

"Yes..." She pulled in a deep breath, then another. "I'm...I'm fine."

"Are you sure?"

"Yes...thank you. I guess the wine just went down the wrong way." Why had he been staring at her like that? Had she done something wrong? Had her thoughts somehow managed to slip out as spoken words? Was he suspicious of her? If he was on to her real intentions, she would never be able to find the answers she needed.

The timer on the microwave signaled that the meals were ready. He took out the trays and placed them on the table. "Dinner is served."

"It smells good." Paige picked up her fork and took a bite of the baked chicken.

Bryce explained the details of his business to his new assistant while they ate, making a concentrated effort to keep his tone and manner impersonal and not stray to other topics. It took more diligence than he had originally anticipated. Paige had managed to capture his senses and captivate his desire quicker than any woman he had ever met. He desperately wanted to reach out and stroke her hair, touch her flawless skin…and taste her lips. It was an urge he fought off. It would never do, putting himself at risk that way when there was so much at stake.

Her comments about ethics and money continued to nag at his consciousness. It had been an odd exchange of words, almost as if she had been challenging him based on some hidden information. Could that have been part of her agenda, what she had been searching for? But for what purpose? He forced his mind back to the business at hand, choosing to save his speculation for later.

"We have four projects that require my personal attention in London. First we have a buyout of a small London publishing company. Next is the merger of my leather-goods factory with a string of small exclusive boutiques in London and Paris where my company will retain an overall fifty-one percent ownership. Then there's a contract for my public relations firm in New York to represent a British import-export company in the United States. The last project is a proposal to provide original works of art from new and promising artists in the States to one of the most prestigious art galleries in London."

As soon as they finished eating, Bryce handed her four file folders. Their hands touched for the briefest of moments, sending a seductive warmth through his body. He abruptly jumped to his feet, clipping his words as he spoke. "I have several things to dictate into my recorder, so while I'm doing that I want you to familiarize yourself with the contents of these files. They'll give you details about the four projects I mentioned."

With that, he turned and hurried to the back of the plane and disappeared into the back cabin. He had to get away from Paige, from the sensual reaction he had to her proximity. He leaned against the closed door and took a deep breath to calm his nerves. He was accustomed to being in charge of everything that went on around him. He did not like this lack of control that jittered around inside him—a feeling he knew was directly attributable to the sudden presence of Paige Bradford in his life. He took another deep breath, but it didn't help. It did nothing to calm his inner turmoil.

He picked up the small recorder and turned his thoughts to the speech he would be making at an upcoming charity event.

Paige stared at the closed cabin door where Bryce had disappeared from sight. He had certainly managed to skillfully sidestep her questions about ethical behavior. She felt a tightening in her throat and an unsettled stirring in the pit of her stomach. She did not know if it was a result of her irritation over his abrupt departure and rude manner or something far more personal.

All of his actions were abrupt. He was obviously a very busy man who simply did not have time for long-drawn-out explanations and conversations, but that did not excuse his curt manner. She allowed herself a huff of indignation. A little common courtesy was not asking too much, even of a busy man.

Her jaw involuntarily clenched for a moment as she tried to banish the strange feelings that had been churning inside her for the past hour. She seemed to be caught between what she *knew* about the Bryce Lexington who hid behind that too-good-to-be-true image he projected to the public and the reality of the dynamic man who had invaded her life like an unstoppable force of nature.

She took a calming breath. It did not help. She took

another deep breath, held it for several seconds, then slowly exhaled. Paige picked up a file folder and tried to concentrate on the documents. She read the first page, then realized she hadn't a clue as to what she had just read. Instead of seeing the words on the page, she saw a vivid likeness of Bryce Lexington. He had managed to have a disruptive effect on her without even being in the same room.

There were several things she did not know about Bryce Lexington the *man* rather than Bryce Lexington the corporate giant, things she wanted to know—things she *needed* to know. And none of them had anything to do with her father, her need to protect the jobs of her father's employees or her chosen mission to expose the unethical side of Bryce Lexington's business practices.

She tried to get rid of those errant bits of curiosity. She already knew quite a bit about him, but she still lacked the proof of his culpability in her father's death. If she could find that proof she could use it to force him to do something honorable, to secure the jobs of her father's employees rather than tossing them out on the street.

She certainly couldn't trust Bryce to do it on his own. She had learned all about trust from her ex-husband...trusting anyone was something that no longer came easily for her. Once trust had been destroyed, rebuilding it was a long process. And it was a process that she hadn't really started to investigate, one that had not been necessary. She had no need to place that type of trust in anyone else. She could take care of herself.

She breathed a little bit easier as she regained control of her wandering emotions. It had only been a fleeting lapse of judgment and she would not allow it to happen again. She had initially been thrown off balance by the overwhelming magnitude of his dynamic presence, the way he had dominated the large office where they met. After all, she was only human, and even though he was the enemy, that did not negate that he was an undeniably sexy and desirable man.

But Paige had it under control now. No doubt about it. From this moment on their relationship would be business only. No more errant thoughts or idle musings for her. Bryce had given her a great deal of material to look over and she was not about to give him any reason to be dissatisfied with her work. This job was the perfect place for her to carry out her plan and she was determined to go through with it. One way or the other, she would make Bryce Lexington pay for what he'd done.

She stared at the file folders he had given her to study. Then the idea popped into her head. At first it was only an inkling, then it exploded into a full-blown plan. One of these files could give her solid proof of his wrongdoing. Four different projects—surely at least one of them would disclose some underhanded dealings on his part? It would give her written evidence of his ethics and what wasn't in the files would be something she could observe firsthand since she would be present at the meetings. It would be a big step in proving Bryce's duplicity.

Her excitement grew as she picked up the folder and began to search the contents for the proof she needed.

TWO

Bryce stayed in the rear cabin and continued his dictation—reports, letters, memos. He finished the last letter then clicked off the recorder as he glanced at his watch. It was almost midnight Los Angeles time. He left the cabin and walked through the plane, coming to a halt next to the table. Paige's head rested on top of the opened file, her eyes closed. Her slow, even breathing told him she was asleep. He stared at her for a moment. The hard edge he had put on his feelings softened as he continued to gaze at her. She was truly lovely. If only he could figure out what was on her hidden agenda.

He carefully picked her up and carried her to the back cabin. She stirred, but only snuggled farther into his arms without waking. It was a small thing, but the intimate gesture touched off a rush of excitement deep inside him. He held her in his arms a moment longer than necessary before gently placing her on the bed. He removed her shoes, then pulled a blanket over her and left the cabin.

Bryce poured himself a glass of wine, then sat at the table, his forehead creased in deep concentration as his thoughts turned to the situation at hand. He pictured the beautiful woman who had snuggled so enticingly in his arms and thought back to her comments about ethical behavior and monetary results. *I don't know what you're up to, Paige Franklin Bradford, but I think finding out is going to be a very interesting adventure.*

An image of Paige appeared in his mind's eye. An uncomfortable shiver made its way up his spine. He wanted to rid himself of the image and everything implied that went with it. He *wanted* to, but he didn't seem to be able to force himself to do it. The delightful image played over and over in his mind.

He knew he needed to be very careful in how he proceeded. If she did, indeed, have some sort of hidden agenda as Joe had suggested, then any misstep on his part would only provide her with more fuel. Bryce had to make sure everything was totally proper and aboveboard—a thought that led him back to his curiosity over her comment about business ethics.

He leaned back in the recliner, closed his eyes and took several deep breaths. He needed to get some sleep. A few minutes later his conscious thoughts were replaced by the subconscious workings of his mind.

The private jet streaked its way eastward through the night sky, eventually traveling into daylight.

Paige woke with a start as the morning sun shone through the window and landed on her face. She sat up abruptly and looked around, trying to get her bearings. She knew she was still on the jet, but did not recall leaving the main cabin. Nor did she remember exactly when she fell asleep, other than the fact that it was somewhere during file number three. Her suitcase sat on the floor by the bed and her shoes were next to it. She took a quick shower. As soon as she finished dressing she went to the main cabin.

She found Bryce stretched out in one of the recliners, his fingers laced together and his hands resting casually across his stomach. He was asleep. He seemed totally and completely at ease. Absolutely no tension showed on his face. She watched him for a moment. She scowled as a twinge of disgust jabbed at her. It was evident that he did not allow his ruthless business tactics to disturb his peace of mind.

As Paige continued to watch him, he began to stir. Suddenly he bolted upright in the chair, instantly wide awake.

"Bradford!" He stared at her for a long moment wondering what had been going through her mind to cause the strange expression on her face. He immediately assumed command of the situation. "Well—" he rose from the chair and stretched his arms above his head "—I see you're finally awake. Maybe now you'll have time to finish going over those files. You seem to have fallen asleep in the middle of number three." With that, he turned and went to the galley to fix some coffee.

"Finally awake?" Her hackles stood on end as she glared at him. She could not prevent the animosity from creeping into her voice. "Just what do you mean by that? You can't expect people to work twenty-four hours a day."

Either he didn't hear her or was purposely ignoring her questions. Either way, perhaps it was just as well. She needed to watch her step. She knew she was in a position to be able to uncover the type of information she needed. She didn't want to do anything to cause him to fire her from this job. Yes, caution was definitely in order regardless of his having just exhibited yet another example of his abrupt behavior.

She backed off for a moment as she watched him. She silently acknowledged that he was fixing the coffee himself rather than expecting her to do it. She tightened her jaw again. That was the only thing she would admit. She retrieved files three and four from the table then sat down on the couch to continue where she had left off before falling asleep.

"Here, Bradford." Bryce set a cup of coffee next to her. "Hurry up and finish with those files. We're landing in an hour." With that, he took his coffee and went into the back cabin.

Paige continued reading the files, closing file number four half an hour later just as he opened the door and came back into the main cabin clean shaven and wearing fresh clothes. She did not entirely understand all the ramifications of his proposal for profits and how they would be allocated, but the amount of notes, including his hand-written notations, indicated to her that the London art gallery was his pet project. She recalled Bryce's degree in fine art, which would account for his interest.

"Any questions, Bradford?"

"None that I can think of right now."

He flashed a quick smile that said he knew better. "There will be." He dismissed the subject as he reached for the coffeepot to refill his cup. He held up the pot in her direction, cocked his head and raised a questioning eyebrow. "Bradford?"

She held up her cup. "Yes, thank you."

It annoyed her, the way he looked as rested as if he had just had eight hours' sleep in a comfortable bed rather than a few hours in a chair. She entertained a brief question as to why he had allowed her to have the bed. She did not remember walking, so he must have carried her into the cabin. It had been a very considerate gesture on his part. She quickly reined in her thoughts. It would take more than one moment of consideration to alter her opinion of him and what he represented.

She wondered what other unexpected thoughts would force themselves upon her as a result of her in-person association with this man—this dynamic and impressive man. In the secret recesses of her mind she began to wonder if she had gotten in way over her head.

"Buckle your seat belt, Bradford. We're approaching the airport."

The jet touched down for a perfect landing. Bryce gathered the files Paige had been reading plus the papers he had been working on and shoved them into a briefcase, then thrust it into her hands.

"You take this, Bradford. I'll get the suitcases."

They exited the plane, cleared customs, then went immediately to the taxi that whisked them into London. Forty-five minutes later he unlocked the front door of an attractive flat in the fashionable Knightsbridge section. After depositing the suitcases on the living-room floor he launched into a quick tour. It was a much larger place than it appeared from the outside.

There were three bedrooms, a large living room, a dining room, kitchen and two bathrooms. "The front bedroom is the largest and is used as an office." He indicated the door, then headed down the hall.

She stuck her head through the opened door to give a quick look, then hurried to catch up with Bryce who was already at the next room.

"This is my bedroom, and that—" he pointed to the next room down the hall "—is the guest bedroom."

Paige really had not formulated any definite thoughts

about sleeping arrangements. Even though Eileen said she would be staying at the corporate flat, it had not occurred to her that they would be sleeping this close to each other. She felt the scowl spread across her face, but was unable to stop it before it caught his attention.

"You look angry. Is there a problem of some sort?"

Paige swallowed the words she wanted to say, instead making an inadequate attempt at covering up. "Uh…no, of course not." She was in a precarious situation. She didn't trust him, but it was not an uneasiness over her physical safety. What she didn't trust was the *concerned good guy* persona he tried to project. But she didn't dare let on…not if she wanted to stay on his good side so she could find the proof she needed.

Bryce's brisk manner gave no indication of his thoughts. "If there's no problem, then let's get to work. As soon as you unpack, I want you to transcribe all the material I dictated on the plane. I've left the tape next to the computer. I'm sure you'll find everything you need in the office." He disappeared inside his bedroom, closing the door behind him.

Paige picked up her suitcase and took it into the guest room as she considered what had just happened. It had been a bad slip to let Bryce see her displeasure. She could not afford for her inner feelings and ulterior motives to seep through. She had to continue to appear as simply another one of his employees. She couldn't risk antagonizing him, at least not until she had what she wanted.

The problem was…well…he had her confused. She knew exactly who and what he was, but he refused to fit into the mold she had created for him in her mind. Yes, indeed—Bryce Lexington had her very confused. And not the least of it was her undeniable attraction to him, an attraction she needed to squash before it caused her real problems. She toyed with the notion that some of her antagonism toward him just might be a defensive mechanism directly related to that attraction.

After unpacking, she went down the hall to the office where she found the tape next to the computer. She listened to the first three letters without transcribing anything, then stopped the tape. He was truly amazing. He dictated as if he were actually reading something—no pauses to think, no changing his mind. She rewound the tape and started from the beginning.

She had barely finished the letters when the phone rang. When it rang a second time without Bryce making an appearance from his bedroom, she quickly grabbed it before it could ring a third time.

"Hello...yes, and who...uh, please hold a moment."

She knocked softly at his bedroom door, her senses still numbed by the identity of the caller—the French ambassador himself, in person rather than his secretary. When she received no response to her knock, she called out to him. "Mr. Lexington...uh, Bryce?"

His voice came from behind the closed door. "Don't stand out in the hall, Bradford. Come on in."

She cautiously opened his bedroom door, not at all sure what she would find. He was turning out to be one surprise after another. Bryce sat on an exercise cycle, pedaling away while reading a book.

"A phone call for you. It's the French ambassador."

He wore only a pair of jogging shorts. His entire body, from his broad shoulders down to the bottom of his long legs, was taut and muscular without being muscle-bound and every bit of exposed skin was as tanned as his face. He obviously spent a great deal of time in the sun.

Paige experienced the same jolt of sensual desire as when they'd first met. Not only was he the most incredibly handsome man she had ever seen, he was an ideal specimen of the perfect male physique. A wave of heated desire swept through her body making it feel as if the temperature in the room had jumped at least twenty degrees. She quickly brought her gaze back to Bryce's face for fear that she might be tempted to mentally remove his jogging shorts.

His expression brightened at the mention of the phone call. He put down his book, then climbed off the exercise cycle. He grabbed a towel and wiped the glistening sheen of perspiration from his face and neck. Without a word to Paige, he picked up the phone extension in his bedroom. A dazzling smile spread across his face. "Andre, *mon ami.*" His entire conversation was in French.

Paige spoke some French, enough to get by, but certainly nothing compared to what she heard coming from Bryce. He spoke rapidly, too rapidly for her to catch all of what he was saying. There was something about having just arrived a few hours ago and an agreement to be somewhere the following evening, then he hung up.

"I hope you brought something formal, Bradford. We're going to a reception at the French embassy tomorrow night."

She stared at him, her eyes wide in amazement. "We're what?"

"You've got to learn to pay closer attention."

"I heard what you said, I just don't believe what I'm hearing. It never occurred to me to pack anything that formal." She made no attempt to hide her irritation, but did try to curb her anger. "You didn't mention anything about me needing something for this kind of event. In fact, you gave no hint of any kind as to what I—"

"You're right. My fault."

"You barely gave me time to pack—" She stopped in

midsentence as the full realization of what he said finally hit her. "What?"

He spoke quietly, his words surrounded by a soft sincerity. "I said you were right. It was my fault. I should have been more specific with my instructions."

Had she heard him correctly? He had readily accepted blame and was that a conciliatory note of apology in his voice? That was most certainly out of character for him, or at least her preconceived notion of who and what he was. What type of underhanded maneuver was he trying to perpetrate? That was the second time he had done something completely out of character. Paige had him neatly categorized and did not like it when he did something contrary to that mold. Well, he still didn't fool her. Two isolated incidents were hardly enough to change her opinion. Bryce was a ruthless business shark who could not be trusted.

"We'll go shopping first thing in the morning to get you something appropriate. Now—" he changed topics without warning, indicating that the discussion about clothes was finished "—how are you coming with my dictation?"

She marveled at the speed with which he moved from one topic to another. Before she could get an answer out, she saw the look in his eyes shift from the current situation to something far removed. He slung the towel around his neck, grabbing the ends where they hung across his chest. He creased his forehead in concentration for a moment as he stared at her, or more accurately, he seemed to be staring *through* her to some unknown spot.

"Tell me, Bradford, do you know how to snow ski?"

"Dictation? Snow ski? Which question do you want answered first?" She tried to put some sense to the way his mind jumped from one thing to another, but it was quickly becoming a formidable task.

"Both of them." He said it as a simple statement of fact, as if he thought it should have been obvious.

She took a calming breath in an effort to combat her rising frustration with what appeared to her to be the disjointed way he jumped from one thing to another without warning. "All the letters and memos have been transcribed and are in the computer. I haven't done the reports or speech yet. Yes, I know how to snow ski."

He offered her a dazzling smile, as if the previous few minutes of tension and the earlier cross words had never happened. "Good. I have business in Aspen at the end of next week. There's still some good spring skiing conditions."

He absently tugged on the ends of the towel, first one end then the other, causing it to slide back and forth across his nape as he stared at the floor deep in concentration. Suddenly he yanked off the towel and tossed it into a basket in the corner. "Transcribe everything except the speech. Hold off on that until tomorrow. I want to give it some more thought. I'm going to take a shower, then we'll get something to eat."

As abruptly as it had all started, their conversation was finished. He went to the bathroom across the hall and closed the door. A few moments later she heard the shower running. Paige could not stop the slight smile that tugged at the corners of her mouth. In spite of his abrupt manner, she had to admit that he was the most fascinating and baffling man she had ever come across. She closed her eyes and pictured his tanned body under the spray of the shower. A jolt of desire swept through her.

What was even more amazing was that he did not seem to have any pretensions about who he was, right down to not seeming to realize just how attractive he was. He sported the trappings of a very busy man and Eileen had warned her about him being a workaholic, but he did not exhibit any ego problems.

What had she gotten herself into? A formal reception the next evening at the French embassy in London and then skiing in Aspen the following week and all as part of her job. Most people would kill to have a job like that, but for her it was only a temporary situation. A means to an end. A little twinge jabbed at her consciousness. She could not clearly identify it. Perhaps it was regret, maybe even guilt. She wasn't sure she wanted to know. She did not want any errant emotions dissuading her from the course she had set.

She finished the reports, then listened to the first part of the speech. She turned off the cassette player and leaned back in her chair. The speech, like the letters and memos, was dictated straight through without pauses. It was an excellent speech, articulate and entertaining while still making the necessary points. She couldn't imagine what there was that he would want to change.

"I've thought about it and won't be making any changes to the speech. You can transcribe it after we get something to eat. Then we'll call it a day."

The sound of his voice startled her, causing her to whirl in her swivel chair. He stood framed in the office doorway wearing only a towel wrapped around his hips. Droplets of water still clung to his tanned skin. His hair had been quickly towel dried and hung in tousled disarray. His turquoise eyes sparkled with life and vitality.

He continued to speak as if he had not noticed her reaction to his sudden appearance. "I imagine you'll be wanting to get a good night's sleep to catch up on the jet lag. Tomorrow is going to be a very busy day, then there's the reception in the evening."

The heat rose on the back of her neck as her heart beat just a little faster and her breathing increased. He looked absolutely gorgeous in a wildly abandoned and totally un-inhibited way. Paige tried to cover the flush of excitement that darted through her body. She swallowed the lump that had lodged in her throat and quickly averted her eyes.

Her words were terse as she turned away from him and went through the motions of shutting down the computer. She knew the quaver in her voice would probably betray her even though she tried to sound in control. "I would appreciate it if you would present yourself properly dressed. Even though this is your residence, it's still a place of business."

In spite of her words she truly believed he was unaware of his state of dress…or more accurately, his state of undress. What she had observed of him so far told her that when Bryce had something on his mind, he acted on it immediately while the thought was still fresh. Even though he had a total grasp on what was happening around him, he seemed to pay no more attention to himself than he did to the wallpaper in the hallway or the air he breathed.

Bryce glanced at the clock on the desk. "We'll leave here in half an hour. There's a little Italian place only a couple of blocks away. We can walk." He turned and went to his bedroom as if her comments about his lack of clothes had not penetrated his consciousness.

Paige leaned back in her chair, closed her eyes, expelled a quick breath and composed her trembling insides. She began to wonder if accepting this job had been a bad idea, not the stroke of luck she had originally thought it to be.

A quick shot of panic raced through her. She needed to escape the mesmerizing aura of Bryce Lexington and the excitement that darted around inside her whenever she looked at him. She shook her head in resignation. As soon as they got back to Los Angeles she would resign from the job. There had to be some other way of digging out the truth about how he ruined her father without being in such proximity to this very disconcerting man.

And whatever it was she had to find it.

She took a steadying breath. She desperately needed to get control of herself. She knew she could not get on with her life until she was able to put to rest the painful chapter concerning her father's suicide. She had to find closure for that traumatic episode and that meant eventually confronting Bryce Lexington. She took another calming breath, turned her attention to putting things away in the office, then went to her room.

It had been an exceptionally long day. Pangs of hunger battled with her yawns for control of her body. Dinner followed by some much-needed sleep were the only two items on her agenda for that night. Perhaps things would be a little clearer in the morning.

And maybe Bryce Lexington would not turn her reality inside out every time he looked at her. A little sigh of despair presented itself. Sure…and maybe some unknown benefactor would drop a million dollars in her lap, too.

She freshened her makeup and changed clothes, selecting a pair of black slacks with a red and white silk blouse and red shoes. The slacks had a matching jacket. An uneasy nervousness churned in the pit of her stomach. Even though she didn't feel any concern for her physical safety, she didn't trust Bryce Lexington any more than she trusted any other man. Trust had to be earned, not freely given.

While waiting for him, Paige took the opportunity to look around the flat a little more thoroughly. She wandered into the kitchen, opening the cupboard and looking into the refrigerator. There was some food, staples only, but not anything that would allow them to have dinner there.

"There'll be some food here tomorrow morning."

Again, the sound of that smooth masculine voice sent

little tingles up her spine at the same time that it startled her to attention. Why did he persist in sneaking up behind her like that? No, that was an unfair statement. Her mind had been absorbed in her own thoughts and she simply hadn't heard him enter the kitchen.

He looked devastatingly gorgeous. He wore a turquoise-blue shirt open at the neck almost the exact color of his eyes and charcoal-gray slacks. Her heartbeat increased ever so slightly. She fumbled for some words, anything that would relieve the tension rapidly building inside her. "Who takes care of this place when you're not here, or do other people also use it?"

"Well, finally a question." He flashed her a dazzling smile. "I was beginning to wonder if you had any curiosity at all." He glanced at his watch. "Let's go, Bradford. I'll answer any questions you have while we walk."

He had done it to her again, abruptly changed everything without warning. Why did he persist in doing that? An abstract thought crept into her mind, though she was not sure exactly where it had originated. Was this his way of testing people? Of determining if someone had what it took to be part of his fast-paced world? If so, it was certainly an interesting method.

Paige gathered her determination. She would show him that she was up to anything he chose to throw her way. She grabbed her jacket, then they stepped outside into the cool night air. He set a brisk pace, but not too fast, as they walked down the tree-lined street.

Bryce willingly filled her in on how the London flat, as well as all the corporate properties, were maintained. "I have a real estate management firm who makes sure the place is cleaned on a weekly basis. The flat is used by various company executives when they're in London on business as well as by a few select clients. Everything is scheduled through Eileen so that there aren't any embarrassing mix-ups. She notifies the management firm and they stock the refrigerator. I was originally scheduled to arrive tomorrow rather than today, thus no food in the refrigerator yet.''

As long as he seemed to be talkative, she ventured another question, one she hoped would lead her to some information about her father. "How many companies do you own? Your business interests, based on the four files you gave me to read, seem to be quite varied.''

Bryce studied her thoughtfully. He wondered why she would be asking something she probably already knew. Well, he could play that game right along with her. If he encouraged her questions, she just might tip her hand as to what she was really looking for. Besides, he didn't have anything to hide.

"Ah, yes. My *mini-empire*.'' He laughed. "You'll find public relations and marketing information about all the companies in the computer. All you have to do is call it up and print it out.''

"You seem to be…well…surprisingly open about your business interests, especially considering that I'm barely more than a stranger to you.''

Bryce stopped walking. He searched the depths of her hazel eyes before speaking. "I like to think that people are basically honest and trustworthy, that they function in an honorable manner.'' He could not stop the tinge of disappointment that surrounded his soft words. "But sometimes things happen that prove me wrong.'' He shifted his gaze off toward the horizon, then started walking again. His thoughts had been about Stanley Franklin. He had not categorized Stanley Franklin's daughter…at least not yet.

"From what you've said it sounds like ethical behavior

is important to you in your business dealings. Does that apply to everything?''

He came to a halt and leveled a serious gaze at her, taking a moment to turn her question over in his mind. It was the second time she had brought up the subject of ethics. Was it a window into her hidden agenda? Something to do with her reason for being there? If it was, he hadn't put it together with a motive yet.

Bryce finally answered her question. "I have a high regard for honesty in everything, not just business." He continued down the sidewalk toward the restaurant.

Paige suffered a quick stab of apprehension as they walked along in silence. Was his answer really a warning aimed specifically at her? Did Bryce suspect she had been lying to him, or was it just a matter of her own guilt bothering her? In spite of the deception she had orchestrated, she was not usually a dishonest person. She shuddered at the contradiction between her actions and her beliefs.

"So…you feel that all business transactions should be conducted with total honesty and in a highly ethical manner?''

"Don't you?''

"That's a very admirable sentiment, but don't you find that occasionally it's just not possible? That sometimes you need to bend the rules a bit in order to get what you want?''

"Rules have the occasional exception," he told her, "but I prefer to trust that most people are honest and ethical.''

"Hypothetically speaking, what would you do if you found yourself involved in a deal and discovered your trust had been misplaced, that the person you were dealing with was unethical and unprincipled?''

Bryce stopped walking again, stared her square in the eyes and gave a straightforward reply. "I'd break off the negotiations.'' Without waiting for her response, he proceeded down the street.

Paige rushed to catch up with him. It was a conversation she was grateful to have ended, even though it was one she had started. There was something about his words that made her regret bringing up the topic of ethics and trust. Bryce Lexington was beginning to seem a little less like the villain she had painted him and more like someone she would like to know. And if the way he made her heart pound and the blood race through her veins was any indication, she wanted to know him intimately...*very* intimately.

She pursed her lips as she tried to get her thoughts back in order. She needed to reaffirm her dedication to her goal. The truth of what really happened between her father and Bryce rested somewhere with Bryce Lexington and she had to find it. Just because he said the right words didn't mean he really lived his life that way.

She clenched her jaw. She didn't believe those words, either. She couldn't trust what he said without some kind of proof. She couldn't trust him. No one who had achieved his level of success did it by always being honest and forthright regardless of his attempt to convince her it was true. She would find the proof she needed and would force him to take care of her father's employees. She would find that chink in his armor no matter what it took to do it.

Three

Bryce and Paige entered a modest building on a quiet side street. It was a charming little Italian restaurant off the beaten path. The aroma of good food floated on the air. Music played softly in the background, just loud enough to be discernible above the buzz of happy and cheerful voices. This was a neighborhood establishment, not one for the tourists.

"Ah...Bryce, my friend!" A short, dark-haired man in his late fifties rushed to them as soon as they came through the door, his thickly accented words leaving no question about his Italian origin.

"It's good to see you again, Antonio. How are you feeling?"

Antonio projected a feigned air of annoyance. "You begin to sound like my wife and children, always asking me how I feel. I feel fine." His voice teased and his dark eyes sparkled as he tapped his hand against his chest. "I am good as a young man of twenty."

Bryce looked around the crowded restaurant, then spoke to Antonio in Italian. Antonio answered him, then signaled a busboy. Paige watched in amazement as a table and two chairs appeared from nowhere and were set up in a quiet corner that just moments before had contained a large potted plant.

She paid close attention to everything. Bryce became more and more puzzling with each new encounter. He seemed to function comfortably on all levels of society—a phone call directly from the French ambassador with a personal invitation to a formal reception and a small neighborhood restaurant owner who called him by his first name while acknowledging their friendship.

Antonio's voice cut into her thoughts. "This way, Bryce—" he stepped aside, waving them in the direction of the table as he smiled at Paige "—and your lovely lady."

No sooner were they seated than a bottle of wine appeared at the table along with menus. Bryce poured them each a glass of wine, then opened the menu. "What's your pleasure, Bradford?"

She looked at the numerous selections. "You seem to know this place very well. Do you have any suggestions?"

"Everything is good. All the pasta is made daily right here in the kitchen and all the vegetables are fresh. Antonio's wife is the cook, his daughter helps with the cooking and fills in as cashier when Antonio isn't here and his sons are the waiters. The entire operation is family run."

A handsome young man of about twenty-two appeared at their table. "Good to see you again, Bryce." He shot a quick look of approval in Paige's direction.

"How are you, Rudy? How's business been?"

The young man laughed, an open and easy laugh. "You should know the answer to that better than I do."

Rudy's words weren't lost on Paige, but she did not understand what they meant.

Bryce quickly scanned the room, then he lowered his voice. "Antonio's been sticking to his reduced work schedule, hasn't he?"

"You know Pop. It's tough to keep him out of here. He's been doing pretty good, though. The doctor says things are just fine." Rudy shot another quick glance in Paige's direction, then leaned over to whisper to Bryce. "It's been a long time since I've seen you with such a foxy lady... someone special, huh?"

He may have been whispering, but it was loud enough for Paige to make out what he had said. She quickly turned away so her embarrassment wouldn't be obvious to everyone. Bryce, on the other hand, did not seem to be embarrassed at all.

"Rudy, this is Paige Bradford. She's a business associate. Bradford, this is Rudy—the youngest of Antonio's five children. He's the least tactful of all the family members...and the biggest flirt." Then, with the swiftness that she was beginning to get used to, Bryce changed the subject. "What's good today, Rudy? Does Maria have something special for a hungry customer?"

Rudy seemed totally unconcerned about the comments concerning his character. "Only a business associate, huh?" He grinned at Paige, then gave her a quick wink before turning his attention back to Bryce. "You're in luck. Mom just finished making some cannelloni." He hurried off toward the kitchen.

"I hope you're hungry, Bradford. Maria doesn't know the meaning of the word *moderate* when it comes to portions of food."

A classically beautiful Italian girl in her early twenties came up behind Bryce, slipped her arms around his neck and kissed him on the cheek. "Papa said you were out here."

"I'd know that sultry voice anywhere." He twisted around in his chair, took her hands in his and extended a warm smile. "Angela, how have you been? Last time I was here you were one month away from motherhood." He slipped his arm around her slim waist and pulled her close to him. His smile quickly shifted to a teasing grin that matched his tone of voice. "Look at this! I can actually get my arm around you now."

"Twins." She beamed at him, her total and complete joy covering her face. "A boy and a girl. We named the girl Sofia, after Grandma. And the boy—" the smile faded from her face and tears formed in her beautiful brown eyes "—we named Bryce…" She quickly blinked the tears away and recovered her enthusiasm. "Bryce Antonio Roberto Vincent—"

"Stop, already!" Bryce broke out in an easy laugh. "The poor kid will be an adult before he gets all of his names memorized."

Paige saw the surprise and the unconcealed emotion dart across his face before he could hide it. She had thought he was merely a good customer over the years, that this very close family were friends of his. But it was now obvious to her that there was more to it than that—much more.

"Bradford, this is Angela. She's the fourth of Antonio and Maria's children. Angela, this is Paige Bradford, a business associate of mine." The two women shook hands.

Angela's enthusiasm bubbled to the surface. "It's time for Papa to go home and rest. If I don't chase him out of here he'll stay until closing." She gave Bryce another affectionate kiss on the cheek. "I'll see you later." She turned her warm smile to Paige. "It was nice meeting you." With that, she hurried off toward the kitchen.

Before Paige had an opportunity to make any subtle inquiries, Rudy returned with the first course of what turned out to be a complete seven-course meal. As Bryce had promised, the food was excellent and there was plenty of it. Somewhere between the fourth and fifth courses Bryce excused himself from the table, saying he wanted to have a word with Maria. She watched as he disappeared into the kitchen.

The fact that he had twice introduced her as a business associate rather than an employee had not escaped her attention. It seemed to demonstrate a sense of equality where others were concerned. It was the same concept as his personal friendship with the French ambassador and also a working-class Italian family who owned a small restaurant. Her preconceived notions about Bryce Lexington were beginning to crumble. Paige was not happy about it, but was not sure how to stop it. She didn't have any idea where to place her trust, that little bit of trust she was able to muster. Should she trust her firmly entrenched beliefs or her subsequent observations of this man?

"Quite a remarkable man, no?" It was Angela's soft voice that captured Paige's attention.

She wasn't sure exactly how to respond to Angela's comment. "He's definitely unlike anyone I've ever met before."

"You're a business associate?" Angela flashed Paige a warm and friendly smile. "So are we. Bryce owns twenty-five percent of this restaurant."

The pride, and it seemed to Paige something almost akin to gratitude, showed on Angela's face. Paige immediately latched on to the twenty-five percent that Angela had quoted. Angela must have been mistaken. A ruthless shark like Bryce Lexington would not be involved in a business if he did not own controlling interest. She tried to maintain a casual tone of voice as she subtly probed for answers. "How did your family come to be in business with him?"

"Bryce had been coming into our restaurant for many years, he knew the whole family. Eight months ago Papa had a heart attack, he needed bypass surgery. Things became very bad financially. Our creditors were after us for past-due bills, we were in danger of losing the restaurant. Then on top of everything else, Grandma became very ill. She was still in Italy. Papa wanted very much to be able to see her before she died but there was no money for a trip and Papa had just had the surgery and all. That was when we became business associates with Bryce."

Angela looked around to make sure no one could hear them. "He took care of all our past-due bills and paid for Papa and Momma to go back to Italy to see Grandma. She died a few days after they arrived. They never would have been able to see her for one last time if it hadn't been for Bryce. When they got back, he sent Papa to a heart specialist in the United States to make sure everything was okay."

"Is that when he took part of your business and made himself your partner?" As soon as the words were out of her mouth Paige wanted to bite her tongue. They sounded too caustic. This young woman obviously thought the world of Bryce, as did her entire family. The last thing she wanted to do was attract undue attention to her real motives and intentions.

Angela cocked her head and creased her forehead for a moment, her expression indicating her confusion over Paige's comments. "Not at all. It was Papa who offered half the restaurant to Bryce to repay the money he had spent on us. Bryce said they would draw up a formal contract for twenty-five percent rather than fifty percent. So far, he hasn't taken any of his profits out of the business. He says we should hold the money in the bank and use it as an emergency fund, in case Papa gets sick again.''

Angela remained for a few minutes longer before hurrying back to work. Paige sat in silence digesting the conversation they had just shared. Was Angela confused about what had happened? The story Angela just gave her did not in any way resemble the actions of a ruthless shark preying on unsuspecting people. Not only had he made his twenty-five percent of the profits available to Antonio as an unrestricted fund, Bryce had reduced Antonio's taxable income by being a partner in the business. This meant that Bryce was actually paying part of Antonio's tax burden.

She didn't know what to make of this new and contradictory information. Could she have been mistaken about Bryce Lexington? She began to wonder if she really knew exactly who and what he was. She clenched her jaw and gathered her determination. No...she was not mistaken. Obviously Angela was the one who didn't have all the facts. Antonio's daughter was far too trusting, the type of mistake Paige would not make for herself ever again.

Bryce emerged from the kitchen a moment later and returned to the table. ''Sorry to be gone so long. I just wanted to tell Maria how much we were enjoying her cooking.'' Somehow she doubted that was what he had really been doing. She suspected he was checking up on Antonio.

Two hours passed before they finally left the restaurant. She was not sure, but it seemed as if there was a bit of a discussion over the bill. As near as she could tell, they did not want to give him a bill, but he insisted on paying. She caught only a bit of what Bryce was saying, his voice teasing rather than chastising. ''How can I expect to receive an accurate accounting of income and expenses when you try to give meals away for free?''

Paige buttoned up her jacket as they stepped outside into the cool night air. It was all she could do to keep her eyes open. She could not remember when she had been as tired as she was at that moment. She paused and took in several deep breaths.

Bryce rushed to her side, concern showing on his face and in his voice. ''Are you all right, Bradford?'' He immediately took her elbow and steered her away from the middle of the walkway.

''Yes, I'm fine. I was just taking in a little extra oxygen, trying to clear my head and wake up. All that food and excellent wine on top of the lack of sleep and suddenly I'm feeling very tired.''

His words were matter-of-fact, his manner all business. ''It's the jet lag catching up with you. As soon as we get back to the flat you go right to bed and get a good night's sleep. You can transcribe the rest of the tape in the morning when you're feeling more rested.''

''I'm sure I'll be fine in the morning.''

''Do you want me to call a taxi?''

''No…thank you. Actually, I'd prefer to walk. I could use the exercise and fresh air.''

''Okay, if you're sure.''

His voice may have taken on a more businesslike tone, but he continued to grasp her elbow in a protective manner as they walked down the sidewalk. Paige found it odd the way the insignificant little gesture seemed to instill in her a feeling of warmth and security. She also found it surprisingly comfortable.

As soon as they arrived back at the flat Paige excused herself and went to her room, leaving Bryce to stand alone in front of his bedroom door. As soon as he was satisfied that she would not be coming back out of her room, he went to his office. Three hours passed with Bryce seated at the computer, staring intently at the screen. He glanced at his watch as he shut down the computer. It was late and there was lots to do the next day.

In addition to the regularly scheduled business, he had to buy Paige something to wear to the embassy reception. A slight smile curled the corners of his mouth. She had been right. He was remiss in not telling her what she would need to pack and she had not been afraid to tell him so. She had an independence he found refreshing. She would certainly be an asset to his company if she were a legitimate employee rather than…a hint of a frown creased his forehead. Rather than what?

He rose from his chair and turned out the desk lamp, then started down the hall. He passed his bedroom and continued, pausing in front of Paige's bedroom. He quietly opened the door just enough to peer inside. He had not heard a sound from her room since they had returned from dinner. He was still a little concerned about her momentary pause, what he had interpreted as a dizzy spell, when they had left the restaurant.

The dim light from the hallway was just enough for him to make out her form as she lay sleeping in the bed. Her auburn hair spread out across the pillow with several strands mussed across the side of her face. He studied her finely sculpted features. Beauty had never taken precedence over brains as far as he was concerned. He wanted a woman with something to offer rather than one who was no more than a decorative accessory.

He had kept a mistress for several years, a discreet arrangement that suited both of their needs. She was an artist who needed a place to work while establishing her career.

He provided her with a studio loft and an income to augment her art sales while she worked to build a following for her work. Neither was interested in taking the relationship further. They had agreed to terminate the arrangement earlier that year and had parted good friends. It was the type of thing that Bryce took great pains to keep out of public knowledge. He firmly believed that his personal life was nobody's business and that included this beautiful woman sleeping in his guest room.

Paige stirred, rolling from her side onto her back. The covers slipped down to her waist. Bryce didn't know if she wore a nightgown or pajamas, but the top was made of some sort of soft-looking, lacy white material that hugged the curves of her body. His breathing quickened slightly. She was a truly complete package—smart, independent and very beautiful. It was a dangerous and highly addictive combination.

Now, if he could just figure out what she was after. Why had she gone to so much trouble to surreptitiously pry into his business and personal life, even to the point of going to work for his company, when she could have just asked him what she wanted to know? Why hadn't she volunteered the information about being Stanley Franklin's daughter when he had interviewed her for the job as his assistant? Why had she asked him what companies he owned when she already knew the answer? And why had she made such a point of bringing up the topic of business ethics and trust? Until he knew the answers to those specific questions and discovered what her hidden agenda consisted of and how it related to him, his best move was to simply play along with her charade even though he found the situation puzzling and the deception uncomfortable.

It had upset him when he heard about Stanley Franklin's suicide, but it hadn't surprised him. Bryce had been amazed that one man could have gotten himself into such a terrible mess through his own misdeeds and bad judgment. He had taken an instant dislike to Stanley Franklin and had washed his hands of the business deal when he had discovered Stanley's illegal dealings. He hadn't really wanted to buy Franklin Industries after Stanley's suicide. He still wasn't sure what to do with the financially troubled company. He estimated it would be operating at a loss for almost five years before the company could be turned into a profitable operation. The subsequent price had been too attractive to resist, but it had not been the major factor in his decision to buy the company.

He watched Paige for a moment longer as she slept. He did not have time in his hectic schedule to concentrate on trying to establish a relationship. He had too many business matters that required his full attention. When he had graduated from college his plan had been to establish his career, then turn his attention to a family. But now…a little sigh of dejection escaped his throat. It seemed to be too late for that. His life was set, his patterns entrenched.

Once again his gaze traced her delicate features and remembered the way she'd snuggled in his arms as he carried her through the plane. He couldn't deny the sensual stirrings that insisted on making themselves known whenever he looked at her. He could not stop the words that came out as a soft whisper. "Good night, Paige." He quietly closed the door to her room.

Paige sat bolt upright and looked around the bedroom, then at the clock on the nightstand. She could not believe how late she had slept. Why had Bryce allowed her to sleep until ten-thirty? She quickly climbed out of bed and grabbed her robe. She was sure he was going to be furious with her and rightfully so. She could not afford to make any mistakes, at least not until she found the proof she needed. She pulled her robe on over her nightgown as she cautiously peered out into the hallway. There were no sounds of any kind and she did not see Bryce.

She hurried to the bathroom and took a shower. Without any wasted moments, she applied her makeup and dressed, then made her way down the hall. She still didn't hear any sounds. Paige checked the office and found it empty. She called his name, but received no response.

Coffee. She smelled coffee. She headed straight for the kitchen. Someone had been there, fresh coffee was waiting and the refrigerator had been stocked. She poured herself a cup of coffee and popped an English muffin into the toaster. An errant thought caused her to chuckle out loud. How could she possibly be thinking of food after that huge dinner she had consumed the previous night?

As soon as she buttered her muffin and poured a second cup of coffee, she went to the office to begin work. She still had the speech to transcribe. She didn't know where Bryce was, but she wanted to make sure the work was completed by the time he returned.

She switched on the computer. The words immediately jumped up in front of her, filling the entire screen. *BRADFORD: COULDN'T WAIT FOR YOU TO GET UP, TOO MUCH TO DO. BE BACK BY NOON.* She glanced at the clock. That was in half an hour. She wouldn't have time to transcribe his speech, but she could get started on it. She took another sip of her coffee, then placed the cassette in the player.

She heard the front door open and close, then his voice was behind her. "Well, I see you finally decided to get up. You can forget that speech. I did it hours ago. Someone had to."

It was worse than she had originally thought. She may

have taken the job under false pretenses, but she had made a commitment to do the work and had accepted the responsibility. She stared at the monitor, too embarrassed to face him. "I'm usually a very early riser. I guess the jet lag got to me, but that's not any excuse for sleeping as late as I did."

She felt torn between her embarrassment over the turn of events and her irritation at him for arbitrarily jumping in and usurping her job. Her better judgment told her to let it drop, but her independent spirit dictated that she have her say in the matter. "You didn't need to do my work for me." Paige took a steadying breath and swiveled in the chair so that she could face him. "All you needed to do was bang on the door to wake me and—"

She stopped short. The teasing grin tugging at the corners of his mouth grabbed her attention. There was no anger in his face. In fact, it was quite the contrary. Amusement crinkled around the corners of his eyes.

It was as if he had not heard a word she had said. He thrust two large sacks at her. "Here, Bradford. Try these on for size."

She stared at the sacks for a moment, then looked quizzically at him. "What's this?"

"Bradford, you've already wasted half a day. Go try it on and stop wasting more of my time." She was not quite sure how to interpret what had just happened. Was he angry with her or teasing her? She had painted him in her mind as such a villain that she was now having difficulty separating her preconceived notions from what was really happening. She took the bags and went to her bedroom.

Paige took the boxes out of the sacks, removed the lid from the largest box and folded back the tissue paper. She stared at the contents in awed silence. It contained a dress, the most stunning evening gown she had ever seen. She carefully picked it up and held it in front of her. It was the most glorious color, a dazzling emerald green. The bodice sparkled with what seemed to be millions of tiny beads. The soft fabric of the dress flowed down to the floor. One side was slit up to the knee.

The gown had long sleeves and was cut high around the neck. Across the front of the upper bodice were five diamond-shaped cutouts that allowed the skin to show through. The cutout in the middle was larger than the two on either side, with the bottom point dipping dangerously low. The back plunged all the way to the waist. Paige had never seen anything like it. She reached into the box and withdrew a matching shawl. The other bag contained a pair of high heels in the same color. She stared at the articles of clothing. The dress was almost too beautiful to touch, let alone wear.

While Paige was in the bedroom, Bryce busied himself in the office checking over the contracts for the purchase of the publishing company. He had an appointment for one o'clock that afternoon to get them signed. After that, he would turn everything over to Ben Jordan, his executive vice president, for any follow-up details and to handle a smooth transition of management.

Following the meeting, he and Paige would need to get ready for the reception. Andre was sending a limo for them promptly at six-thirty. Bryce put the last of the papers in his attaché case and glanced at his watch.

Her soft voice contained just a hint of huskiness as it captured his attention. "It's a beautiful dress, and it fits perfectly."

As Bryce turned toward her he felt briefly disappointed. Paige had changed back into the clothes she had been wearing earlier. Apparently, he would not get to see her in the dress until that evening. "I'm glad you like it. Did everything fit okay?"

"Everything. How did you do it?"

"Simple, Bradford. I just told the saleslady I wanted a dress to fit someone five feet seven inches tall whose measurements were a perfect 36–24–35 in American inches. She converted that to European standards, and there you have it."

Paige flushed with embarrassment. She stared at the floor, unable to maintain eye contact with Bryce. He may have said it as a plain statement of fact, but it left her feeling weak. She had no idea he had such a discerning eye or that he had looked her over that closely. He certainly had not been obvious in his visual survey.

"Bradford, you're bright red!" Bryce blurted out the words, his genuine surprise carrying in his voice as well as showing on his face.

Paige certainly did not want to discuss her embarrassment. "Uh, the shoes. Even the shoes fit perfectly."

"That was easy." He reached over to the chair and picked up the shoes she had worn the previous evening. "You left these in the living room last night. I took them with me." He glanced at his watch, all business again as he picked up his attaché case. "Come on, Bradford. We have a one o'clock meeting."

The afternoon went quickly with Bryce taking masterful control of the meeting. As soon as everything was signed they returned to the flat to get ready for the reception at the French embassy.

Paige spent an hour and a half doing her hair and makeup. She wanted everything to look perfect, as perfect as the gorgeous dress she would be wearing. She finally slipped into the dress, then studied her reflection in the full-

length mirror. She was satisfied with what she saw. Her
hair was done in an upswept style with coiled wisps feath-
ered around her face. There was nothing left except the
shoes. A few minutes later she stepped into the living room.

"Well, I guess I'm ready." She detected the nervousness
in her voice as she spoke, a nervousness accentuated by the
sight of Bryce standing by the front window wearing his
tuxedo. She was sure a more handsome, debonair man did
not exist.

She offered him a tentative smile as he turned toward
her. "I've never been to an embassy reception." She
twirled in a quick circle, then faced him again. Her words
were hesitant. "Do I look okay?"

Bryce literally experienced a shortness of breath as he
watched her twirl around. She was the most exquisitely
beautiful woman he had ever seen. The dress fit her perfectly. The bottom point of the center diamond cutout
showed just enough cleavage to be enticing while still allowing her to look every bit the classy lady she was.

The dynamic Bryce Lexington was seldom at a loss for
words, but this was one of those rare occasions. He couldn't
force any sounds past the lump in his throat. He was unable
to take his eyes off her. She sparkled and dazzled as bril-
liantly as the bits of glitter sprinkled in her glossy auburn
hair. His pulse rate doubled—at least. With a great deal of
difficulty he finally found his voice.

"Bradford, you look…" He searched for the proper
word, something that conveyed how breathtakingly incred-
ible she looked without sounding so personal that his words
would betray the sensual desire the churned inside him. He
was acutely aware of how often his thoughts had strayed
from the business to the personal where she was concerned
and it bothered him more each time it happened. No matter
how tempted he was to pursue his desire for this very al-

luring woman he knew it would not be a wise move, at least not until he had determined exactly what she wanted from him.

He noted the anxious look on her lovely face, the way her eyes seemed to be asking for his approval. It was the first crack he had seen in her confidence, the first sign of any uncertainty. He finally managed a weak, "You look very nice," even though he knew the words were woefully inadequate.

The limo arrived. Bryce draped the shawl around her shoulders and they left, arriving ten minutes later at their destination.

The French embassy glowed, not only from the thousands of lights but also from those assembled at the stellar gathering. Paige, too, seemed to glow with excitement. Bryce had not said too much in the limo. He was still wrestling with his thoughts and feelings, which continued to do battle with the logical and pragmatic businessman in him.

Personal relationships devoid of any business purpose were something that he had never had time for. His life was already busy and his schedule very full. He knew it would take a very special woman to fit into his world and as of yet he had not found her. Nor had he found someone for whom he would be willing to alter his hectic lifestyle.

He stole a furtive glance toward Paige. A warm feeling settled inside him. If only he knew what was on her agenda, why she had decided to insert her presence into his life and what she ultimately wanted from him. It thrilled him to see the glow of excitement on her face as she looked around the room.

Paige had never seen such a glittering array. Champagne flowed, the sounds of the orchestra filled the ballroom and filtered into the surrounding rooms and out to the terrace.

The buffet table contained every conceivable type of food. As much as she tried to be very sophisticated and blasé about the entire event, she could not contain her exhilaration. It filled her to the point of blocking out any and all preconceived notions about Bryce.

Only fifteen minutes after they arrived, just long enough to go through the receiving line, Paige encountered one elegantly attired man after another who asked her to dance. At first she was hesitant, not certain what her obligation was to Bryce as her escort, but he insisted that she go and enjoy herself. After that, she graciously accepted all dance invitations.

Even though Bryce moved effortlessly from one conversation to another, from one group of people to another, he never lost sight of Paige. She was the most captivating woman in attendance. Her smile enchanted everyone who was lucky enough to fall within its spell. Her laugh rivaled the sweetest music. Her eyes sparkled. Very unnerving sensations tugged and pulled at his insides—sensations centered around Paige Bradford, sensations he didn't seem to have any control over, sensations that left him with an unaccustomed and unacceptable feeling of helplessness.

The evening was a rousing success. It was well past midnight and at least half of the guests were still dancing and enjoying the party. Bryce picked up two glasses of champagne and made his way across the room just as the orchestra finished its song. Before someone else could ask Paige for the next dance, Bryce intervened. Handing her a glass of champagne, he indicated the opened door leading out to the terrace. "How about a breath of fresh air?"

She shot him a grateful look and a sincere smile. "I could use some. Not only have I been on my feet since we arrived, my poor feet have been in brand-new shoes." She turned and glanced out the door. "Do you suppose there might be a chair out there?"

"I'll bet we could find one." He offered her a dazzling smile. "Come on, let's take a look." He placed his hand at the small of her back and guided her through the door to the terrace. It was a beautiful night. The dark sky twinkled with a million stars, the full moon shone like a giant silver ball hanging high above the horizon.

"Here we go," Bryce held a chair for her. "Two chairs and even a table."

Paige immediately sank into the seat and set her glass of champagne on the table. A quick sigh of relief escaped her lips as she closed her eyes for a moment and allowed a smile of pleasure to curl the corners of her mouth. "It feels so good to sit down." She slipped her feet out of the shoes, then bent over to massage one foot. "My feet aren't accustomed to this much abuse."

Bryce set his glass on the table next to hers, then moved the other chair so that he sat facing her. "Here—" he motioned for her to extend her foot toward him "—let me do that for you."

She leaned back in her chair, closed her eyes and allowed the feeling of utter contentment to settle over her. He massaged the ball of her foot, then her instep, gradually moving up to her ankle. His sensual touch sent tingles of delight through her body. Her breath quickened, her heart thumped a little faster.

She knew she should not be letting him massage her sore feet. It put too much of a personal twist on things. It detracted from her determination to fulfill her vow to unmask him...but it felt so good. He released her right foot, took her left foot in his hands and started all over again.

It had been the most spectacular evening she had ever spent anywhere. Everything was so exciting and new. The people she met were dynamic, powerful and very charming—just like Bryce Lexington. She was beginning to see through that brusque exterior he presented. The man who had rescued an Italian family from financial ruin and then refused to take his profits was not an ogre. The man who had shown such concern when she paused for some fresh air while leaving the restaurant was not a cold ruthless business shark. And the man who had gone out and personally bought her a dress and was now rubbing her sore feet certainly did not fit the mold of the villain she had created in her mind.

But exactly what was he? She had very mixed feelings. She wished she knew what had happened between him and her father. Did she dare ask him directly? She had originally decided against that plan of action for fear he would quickly cover his tracks and destroy any evidence. Now she did not know what to think. Maybe she should change her mind and just ask him about her father. Some of the ebullience from the evening's festivities that only moments before had filled every corner of her consciousness began to fade. She was not sure what to do. So she did nothing. Somewhere deep inside her flickered the notion that she just might be afraid of what the truth could turn out to be.

He released her left foot. "There…is that better?"

"Mmm…" She opened her eyes and gave him a warm smile while wiggling her toes. "Much better. Thanks." Filtering out to the terrace from inside the ballroom, the soft light highlighted his handsome features. The full moon bathed the gardens with a silvery light that enveloped everything it touched in a magical aura, while the strains of a slow song drifted through the air.

He rose from his chair and held out his hand, his turquoise eyes sparkling in the moonlight. His soft voice floated toward her. "Do you think your feet can handle one last dance before we leave?"

She returned his look, their gazes locking in a brief instant of sizzling intensity. The softness of her voice matched his. "Yes, I think so." She accepted his hand, slipped her feet back into her shoes and stood up.

With smooth perfection Bryce pulled Paige into his arms and began to move with the music. He slid a hand across her bare back, reveling in the silky feel of her skin. She felt good in his arms. He frowned a little. Perhaps she felt too good. He wanted to pull her tightly against his body, to feel her contours molded to his. He wanted to kiss her. He wanted that and so much more, but he managed to curb his impulses. He held her not too tightly and moved to the music.

Paige's insides fluttered in wild abandon. She kept trying to tell herself it was the champagne and the setting that made her feel the way she did, but she knew it wasn't true. Bryce was the cause and it did not matter how much she denied it to herself it was still true. Facts were facts. He excited her in a way that no one else ever had. She wanted him to hold her closer, she wanted to rest her head on his shoulder, she wanted...

She wanted to get the tenuous hold she had on her emotions under tighter control before she made a complete fool of herself. This was business, nothing more. And her business was to find the truth about what happened. She had been taken in before by a man she had trusted, a man who had ultimately betrayed that trust. She would not let it happen again. She needed proof, not the soothing words of a sexy man.

Paige lost herself in Bryce's smooth dance steps. Regardless of her intentions, she momentarily succumbed to the night, the music and the magnetic pull of this totally unacceptable but irresistible man.

The music stopped, but Bryce continued to hold her in his arms and move to the melody that still played in his mind. Then it happened. Paige tilted her head back and gazed up at him as he looked into her face. Her slightly parted lips and lush mouth were too tempting. He could not have stopped the kiss even if he had wanted to. After only the briefest moment of hesitation his mouth found hers. Bryce brushed his lips lightly against hers before sliding his mouth fully onto her lips. She tasted of champagne and earthy sensuality…and he wanted more.

Four

"**Ah**, there you are."

Andre's voice forced the music from Bryce's head. He reluctantly turned Paige loose and stepped back from her.

"Your limo is waiting." Andre's dark eyes twinkled as he looked at Paige, then at Bryce. "Of course, I'm sure your driver would not mind waiting a little longer."

"No. It's late." He glanced at Paige, then returned his attention to Andre. Once again the businessman took charge of the moment. "We have a busy workday tomorrow. Come on, Bradford. Let's go."

Bryce extended his appreciation to Andre for the evening, then hustled Paige into the limo. Neither of them said anything on the short ride back to the flat. He mumbled a weak *good-night* to Paige, then went immediately to his bedroom and closed the door. She stifled a yawn and went to her bedroom. Ten minutes later she climbed into bed.

Paige snuggled beneath the covers, the warm glow of the

party still clinging to her senses and Bryce's brief kiss emblazoned on her lips. It was wrong. He was the enemy yet she had allowed him—*allowed*…she had practically begged him—to kiss her. The line between her determined goals and her newly inflamed desires was becoming more obscure with each passing minute. And she didn't know exactly how to handle it.

It had been the most glorious party of her life. She had taken a minute to stare at her reflection in the mirror before taking off the dress. Wearing it made her feel so special. Paige had quickly put on her nightgown, pulled on her robe and gone across the hall to the bathroom to wash off her makeup and comb out her hair. She knew it was time to leave the world of fantasy and dreams behind and return to the world of reality. Bryce was right, they had a very busy day ahead of them.

She lay in bed staring up toward the ceiling through the darkness, too excited to go to sleep. She didn't want to close her eyes because each time she did she saw Bryce's face clearly etched into the screen of her mind. She had not wanted their dance to end and had certainly not wanted the kiss to end. Nor had she wanted to leave the warmth of his arms. Her own exhaustion finally took control and she drifted into a restless sleep, the very real awareness of his sensual touch complicating the obsession of her original quest.

Unlike Paige, Bryce was awake—wide awake. He did not know whether to be unhappy with Andre for interrupting them or thankful that fate had intervened and prevented him from doing something even more foolish than he already had like holding Paige closer and kissing her very tempting mouth with far more passion than he had allowed. That had been the direction he was headed, as much as he did not want it to be so. He wanted to take her hand, lead her out into the moonlit garden, wrap her in his embrace and never let go.

But right now what he wanted to do was stop the ridiculous thoughts and get some sleep. He had already done enough damage. If Paige did have her own personal agenda as Joe insisted, then he had played right into her hands. That kiss could provide her an excuse to slap him with a sexual harassment suit against the corporation. Bryce's instincts told him that wasn't the case, but logic said he needed to keep his libido zipped up at least until he could figure out what was going on.

He finally fell into an uneasy sleep and endured a restless night.

The next morning Bryce woke early. Today they would be dealing with the art gallery project and there were still several details to be ironed out. He did not have full agreement from all the gallery partners concerning his proposal for allocation of profits. He wanted a certain percentage of gross profits set aside for art scholarships to be awarded to gifted and promising students. The gallery partners wanted a lesser percentage of the net profits set aside. It was a project about which he felt very strongly.

He spent three hours early that morning trying to rework the figures into some sort of compromise. As he carried his third cup of coffee from the kitchen to the office, he detoured down the hall and banged on Paige's closed bedroom door. "Bradford! We've got a lot of work to do."

She responded immediately. "I'll be there in just a minute." Her voice sounded alert and awake from behind the door. A moment later the door opened and she emerged into the hallway. "Good morning." She offered him an almost shy smile. He had been so busy with his project that he had not been aware that she was up.

"You look well rested, did you get enough sleep?" All

the feelings from the night before flooded through him. Her shy smile touched a place of caring and ignited a soft warmth deep inside him.

"I slept very well, thank you." Paige had hoped in the clear light of day things would be different, that she would only be concerned about the business at hand, but she was wrong. All the magic of the night before welled inside her as soon as she heard his voice, as soon as she saw him. "It was a lovely party. Thank you for including me in your invitation."

Bryce tried to sound casual. "Well, I couldn't let you sit here all alone." The slight huskiness in his voice betrayed the true nature of his feelings. He attempted to cover it by quickly putting things back on a business footing. He picked up a file folder and turned toward the computer. "Let's get to work, Bradford."

Paige glanced awkwardly at the floor, then looked up again. "I'll just grab some coffee, then I'll be ready." She hurried toward the kitchen and returned a minute later with a full cup.

The next two hours passed very quickly. The conversation was kept strictly business as they worked diligently to be done by the eleven o'clock meeting with the gallery owners. By ten-thirty, everything had been completed, Bryce's counterproposal was printed out and ready to present. Then, he called for a taxi. They arrived at the gallery right on time.

Paige watched as Bryce took control of the meeting from the outset. All opposition to his revised proposal was swiftly quelled when no better proposal was available. Bryce was masterful. He carefully orchestrated every facet of the meeting and left the gallery partners feeling privileged to even be associated with a Bryce Lexington project. Paige's initial reaction to his revised proposal and his handling of the meeting gave her the impression that he was manipulating the gallery partners into going along with what he wanted…that he had imposed his will on them in order to get his way without regard for their needs.

A quick flash of satisfaction rippled through her. She had finally found something that confirmed her original opinion of this very disconcerting man, that chink in his armor she had been seeking. But then everything turned around on her when she realized that the revised proposal he had pushed so hard to have accepted sacrificed some of his personal profits in order to maintain the standards and integrity of the art scholarships. The scholarships were obviously that important to him.

Her erroneous conclusion only left her more confused about Bryce than she had been before. She tried to keep her attention focused on the conversation detailing the rest of the negotiations, but found that her thoughts kept wandering. Who was the real Bryce Lexington? Was he the man she had determined him to be before she met him or the man she had since observed? And what about her father's company? What were Bryce's plans for Franklin Industries and more importantly for the employees? She wasn't sure what to think anymore. Could she trust what she had observed to represent the real Bryce or was it only a slick facade that hid the truth from view?

Another meeting successfully concluded. Bryce was pleased that everyone was satisfied with the outcome. They had worked through lunch and now it was late afternoon. Neither he nor Paige had eaten anything for breakfast beyond some coffee. Bryce glanced down the street as they emerged from the art gallery.

"Come on, Bradford. It's too late for lunch and too early for dinner, but I'm hungry. How about you?"

"I am a little hungry. I could probably wait until dinner,

but maybe a little something now to hold off the hunger pangs?''

"There's a nice little pub a block from here." He set a brisk pace as they walked to the corner, then entered the pub. They ordered a light snack.

Their conversation centered around the remaining projects and the preparations that needed to be completed before the meetings. Once again he was nonstop energy, not giving her the opportunity to dwell on her speculations or private concerns about Bryce Lexington and what he had in store for her father's company and the employees.

He flagged down a taxi and they returned to the flat. As she exited from the vehicle she tripped and fell to the sidewalk. Bryce rushed to her side and helped her up. A sense of urgency colored his words. "Are you all right, Bradford?"

"Yes, I'm fine." Once again the heat of embarrassment flushed across her cheeks. She avoided his gaze by brushing some dirt from the leg of her slacks, then she noted the slight tear in the fabric. "I'm not normally this clumsy."

"Are you sure you're okay?"

"Yes, honest. The only damage is this little rip in my slacks and a bit of a blow to…" She looked up into a face covered with genuine concern, a look that sent a little tremor of emotion through her body. Her words trailed off in a whisper. "…to my pride."

"When we get back to Santa Monica turn in a bill to Eileen for the cost of your damaged clothes and the company will reimburse you."

"Oh, I couldn't do that. These aren't new and it's a very small—"

His brusque, businesslike manner returned as he escorted her up the walkway to the front door of the flat. "There's still some work to do before we're through for the day, Bradford.''

"Yes, of course." Paige went immediately to the office to enter the notes on the day's meeting into the computer and bring the various files up to date. She allowed a slight grin to tug at the corners of her mouth as soon as she was out of his sight. She had seen the concern written all over his face, had heard it in his voice. She was no longer going to be fooled by that brusque exterior that he seemed to turn on and off at will. It was almost as if he used it as a facade to hide behind. Was she finally beginning to see beyond that barrier? A hint of trepidation told her she might not want to dig any farther into his personal life for fear of what she might find. She turned her attention to the computer and the work that needed to be done.

While Paige updated the files, Bryce changed his clothes, poured himself a glass of wine and slumped into the easy chair in the living room. His thoughts were not on business. He did not know where this relationship with Paige was headed, if indeed it even was a relationship. Did she have any personal feelings about him or were her interests purely business and exactly what was the business that had brought her into his life? He remained lost in his thoughts, his glass of wine untouched.

An hour later Paige emerged from the office, her words drawing him out of his thoughts. "I've finished updating the files. Is there anything else you need tonight?"

"No...nothing. I think we can call it a day...as far as work is concerned." He rose from the chair. His voice softened to a much more personal level. "Would you like to join me for a glass of wine?"

She answered without hesitation. "That would be very nice, thank you."

Bryce poured a glass for Paige, then retrieved his full

glass from the end table. The relaxed, comfortable nature of the evening bewildered Paige even more. The magic of the embassy reception still enveloped her senses, only to be heightened by the abbreviated kiss they had shared on the embassy terrace. As much as she loved her father and as painful as his suicide had been, she could not deny the feelings growing inside her—strong feelings for Bryce. There had to be facts, something that she was not yet aware of, that would explain everything. She needed to know, she had to have all the pieces so she could put the matter to rest. She needed facts, something tangible. She could not trust the intangible.

Their conversation remained light and superficial. She wanted to talk about her father's company, but didn't know how to bring up the subject. As the hour grew later, it was Paige who made the first move to end the evening.

"I think I'd better turn in now."

As she rose to her feet, Bryce captured her hand. His steady gaze searched her face for a brief moment, then plumbed the depths of her eyes before he spoke. "Are you sure you're all right? No lingering problems from your fall?" He continued to hold her hand, the warmth of her skin sending an unexpected surge of delight through him.

Paige squeezed his hand as she gave him a reassuring smile. "I'm just fine, honest." She sucked in a quick, hard breath that was followed by a very noticeable increase in her pulse rate. He made no move to release her hand and she made no effort to remove it from his grasp.

All the magic of the moonlit terrace at the French embassy stirred inside her, engulfing her in a sensual cloud. She again heard the music floating on the air, could almost feel the sensation of his hand sliding across her bare back as they slowly danced in each other's arms.

As if he had been reading her mind, he pulled her to

him, slipped his arms around her and began to move to the music that continued to play through her mind—the same song they had danced to the night before.

It was all she could do to keep from melting in his embrace. She had never felt this way before. She closed her eyes and moved with him. In her mind they were back on that beautiful terrace bathed in the silver glow, a place where time had managed to stand still if only for a few minutes. The line between reality and delicious fantasy started to fade. She nestled her head against his shoulder and allowed him to envelop her.

They slowly danced in each other's arms, moving to the silent music. Time lost all meaning and all reality. It could have been five minutes or it could have been two hours— neither of them knew, neither of them cared.

Bryce reached his fingertips under her chin and lifted her face. It felt so right holding her in his arms again. Their being together felt so very right. He slowly lowered his mouth to hers. All the feelings and emotions he had carefully stored away inside himself over the years flowed to Paige through his kiss. He had not intended to kiss her. He simply could not stop himself. It was something similar to kinetic energy—once it had started, the action moved forward under its own volition. Her lips were soft, her mouth sweet. What began as a tender kiss quickly escalated as his aroused passions came to the surface. He wanted all of her.

Paige had not been prepared for his decision to kiss her. It was wrong, things should be strictly business. He was the man who had been the center of her vendetta for six months. He was the man she believed was responsible for her father's suicide. He was the man who had the power to put one hundred people out of work with the stroke of a pen—one hundred people who had families to support— by simply closing down her father's company.

His kiss deepened and her thoughts and fears melted away in a burst of incendiary desire as she responded to his sensual mouth and the fire that burned inside her.

Bryce forced himself to break off the kiss he had initiated. He cradled Paige's head to his shoulder for a moment as he took a calming breath, then he stepped back from her. Her kiss-swollen lips parted slightly as she looked into his eyes, bewilderment evident on her beautiful face.

He finally found his voice. "It's late, Bradford. Go to bed. We have an early appointment in the morning."

A shaken and confused Paige turned and hurried to the guest room as tears formed in her eyes, hurt and humiliation coursing through her. Her thoughts were on Bryce as she sat on the edge of the bed. She closed her eyes and touched her fingertips to her lips. She still felt the power and passion of his kiss. He had touched the very depths of her soul, stirred passions she had forgotten she even possessed. Why had he so suddenly pulled away from her and dismissed her as if nothing had happened? Unlike the embassy reception where Andre had interrupted them, there had been no reason for his sudden change.

The sound of his voice from the other side of the door interrupted her thoughts. His words were soft.

"Bradford…are you awake?"

She hesitated a moment before answering. "Yes."

"I…I want to apologize for what just happened. I had no right to put you in that position. Making passes at my female employees is not the way I conduct my business and it's not part of your job description."

There was a very brief moment of silence, then he spoke again. "Good night, Bradford." She heard him walk down the hall, then heard his bedroom door close.

* * *

Bryce lay in bed with his hands behind his head, staring up at the ceiling. The look of hurt that darted across Paige's face when he had told her to go to bed had stabbed at him. He had seen the moisture glisten in her eyes before she turned her head away. He heaved an audible sigh of despair. He had hurt her. He had not wanted to, but he knew he had to stop what was happening before it got too far out of hand...while he was still able to stop. He desperately needed to sort out his feelings about her.

Sort out his feelings—that was easy to say, but not so easy to do. This was not a business matter that could be controlled in a cool, logical manner or a compromise to be figured out and negotiated. His feelings and emotions had never been so out of control like this before—at least not this type of emotion. He had never felt so emotionally connected to a woman.

He had never been so confused about anything in his entire life. He had only met Paige a few days ago. He still had no idea why she had made it a point to become involved in his life. He did not know what she wanted from him and he had compounded that by making a pass at her while she was in his employ and staying under his roof for business purposes. Had he created a legal nightmare for himself?

Bryce finally drifted into a fitful night's sleep and woke early the next morning. He had problems to deal with, problems not connected with the London projects or with Paige's presence in his life. He placed a call to his corporate headquarters and talked to Eileen Draper, then Joe Thompkins.

"Anything I should know about, Joe?"

"We've resolved the theft problem at the San Diego facility." An amused chuckle traveled the phone line from Los Angeles to London as Joe provided Bryce with the information. "Actually the situation resolved itself."

"How so?"

"It wasn't so much a theft problem as it was a new employee who was a little overanxious. It seems he was unpacking incoming shipments of office supplies, computer supplies and kitchen supplies before they could go through proper inventory channels. The receiving department showed the boxes arriving, but the items never hit the inventory lists. What the office manager thought was missing turned out to be neatly stored in a supply closet."

"It would be nice if they were all that easy."

"So tell me, Bryce…how are things progressing with the Paige Bradford situation? I haven't been able to uncover any additional information beyond what I gave you before you left for London."

"As far as being an employee, she's excellent. She works hard and is extremely competent and doesn't seem to get flustered in trying to deal with my hectic work habits."

Joe laughed good-naturedly. "Well, that's a big plus for her."

"As far as her motive for being here at all, I don't know any more than I did. There were two or three times when she initiated a conversation about business ethics and trust. I'm not sure what the purpose was or where she had intended to go with it."

"Well, watch your step with her. Don't put yourself in a position where you could end up compromising yourself and the corporation."

The two men touched on a couple of other minor business problems, then terminated the phone conversation. Joe's sage advice was a little too late. Bryce had already put himself in a position where he could end up with a legal problem…the moment he brushed his lips against Paige's on the terrace at the French embassy.

Bryce glanced at his watch, then turned his attention to the financial report that had been sent to him via fax. He was vaguely aware of the sound of footsteps in the hallway, but kept his attention riveted to the business at hand.

Paige stood at the door of the office. She noted the intense expression on his face as he stared at the sheet of paper, his features showing a combination of determination and anger.

"Good morning." Her words were hesitant. It was a very awkward situation. His entire demeanor had changed so abruptly following their kiss the previous night that she was not sure exactly how things stood between them in spite of what he had said after she had gone to her bedroom.

A smile spread across Bryce's face as he swiveled around in his chair. "Good morning, yourself. Are you ready for a busy day?"

His upbeat attitude confused her, especially after the night before. He was acting as if nothing at all had happened. Perhaps that was the best way to proceed—put everything firmly back on a business footing. Paige returned his smile. "I'm ready for anything."

Bryce cocked his head and allowed his gaze to drift from her face to the curves of her body, then back to her face as decidedly erotic thoughts danced through his mind. She was lovely, dressed in a simple pair of slacks and a blouse with her hair pulled back at her nape and fastened with a gold clasp. He saw the nervousness in her eyes, a hint of tension belied by her dazzling smile. And her mouth, her very kissable mouth that tasted sweeter than anything he had ever—

He quickly shook the thought away and returned to business matters. "Today we tackle the merger with the Jean Paul boutiques. The first meeting is at ten o'clock. Here's what I need you to do..."

The day was, indeed, very busy. Neither of them made mention of what had happened the night before. They visited three different boutique locations, then went to the London business offices of the Paris-based company. Once again, Bryce was masterful in his handling of the business arrangements.

Besides being a busy day, it turned out to be a long day. It was a little past seven o'clock that evening when they finally arrived back at the flat. They went immediately to the kitchen where they made quick work of dinner.

"Well, Bradford, only one more to go. Tomorrow morning we'll deal with the contracts for marketing and consulting services with The Brighton Group. Then…" Bryce seemed to lose his train of thought as he looked into her eyes. He hesitantly reached out and lightly stroked her cheek with his fingertips. His voice contained a hint of huskiness. "—then tomorrow evening, if you'd like, we can go to the theater." His manner snapped back into business mode. "It will be a reward for several days of hard work."

Paige felt herself again being drawn into the sensual aura that personified him. Her insides trembled when he touched her cheek. The intensity of his gaze seemed to peer into the depths of her soul. Her knees felt weak. "I'd like that very much." She didn't know what to make of his blunt mood changes. One minute he was soft and caring and the next minute he was all business. She didn't know what to make of her own feelings, either. They concerned and frightened her. With each passing minute she seemed to move farther and farther away from her original plan.

The atmosphere had become decidedly personal. They lingered over a glass of wine, talking comfortably about numerous topics—the theater and which play she would like to see, music, travel and art. She still found it such an odd combination, his intense interest in art and his amazing business acumen.

Did he have a personal art collection, things that could easily be in a museum? Their art gallery meeting had shown her how eclectic his artistic tastes were. His interests tended toward new artists working in a variety of mediums. She hadn't noticed any evidence of a collection at his Santa Monica corporate offices or in the London flat. But then, as he had mentioned, he didn't spend much time in either place. Perhaps in his home. She decided not to ask. It seemed to her that it would be prying into his personal life.

A sharp twinge of guilt jabbed at her. She had already dug into Bryce's life, invading his privacy without regard for his feelings in order to satisfy her own personal goals. All that prying had gotten her nowhere. She had not turned up one negative thing about him or his business dealings. And now that she was in a position to see firsthand how he conducted business, it had only reinforced what she had found out rather than verify what she wanted to believe.

"The Aspen business trip is related to the gallery project." Even though he was imparting business information, his manner was of a much more personal nature. His voice was soft and caring, almost intimate, yet at the same time she felt as if he was studying her.

"We'll be looking at the work of two artists who were brought to my attention. I want to see if their work is appropriate for the London gallery. One of the artists is a sculptor who works primarily with metals. The other works in watercolor and has been doing some very innovative things in that field." His face showed his excitement and she could hear the genuine enthusiasm in his voice as he talked.

The evening settled into a comfortable manner yet there was an underlying current of pent-up desires and emotions that refused to stay buried. Sexual tension sizzled in the air, crackling with a new intensity.

Bryce turned on the stereo and a second later soft music filled the air. He held out his hand toward Paige. "May I have this dance?" It was probably a very bad idea, but Bryce's desires overrode his common sense. He folded her in his arms and they moved to the melody. It felt so very right to hold Paige in his arms. She felt so right that it frightened him. Things were happening too fast. For a man who was used to being in total control of everything around him, he had somehow slipped into a situation where he felt as if he had no control at all.

This time it was Paige who broke off the intimate feeling building between them. "It's late. I think we'd better call it a night." A hint of huskiness surrounded her words.

The disappointment filtered through his consciousness, but the logical side of him said she was right. He took her hand and walked with her to her bedroom door.

"Good night. I'll see you in the morning." He hesitated a moment, leaned in to kiss her far too tempting mouth, then pulled her into his embrace. It was a kiss that nearly destroyed his last vestige of control, a kiss that demanded more than he knew was prudent under the circumstances.

Five

The morning meeting with The Brighton Group had gone exactly as Bryce had wanted it to. Following the meeting he and Paige stopped for a quick pub lunch on the way back to the flat. There was some cleanup work to be done on the gallery project, then Bryce's business in London would be concluded and they would fly back to Los Angeles.

"Bradford, take this information and incorporate it with the existing material, then enter it into the computer files. And while you're doing that..." He paused as he watched her preparing to log on to the computer, his mind momentarily lost in personal thoughts about where the previous evening could have gone...where he had wanted it to go. He quickly regained his composure. "I'll go pick up the theater tickets for tonight."

She turned to face him and smiled, a somewhat distracted

smile due to her concentration on the computer. "I should have this finished by the time you return."

"Good. I'll see you in a bit." He grabbed his jacket and left.

Paige turned her attentions to the work at hand. She quickly finished what Bryce had requested, then paused before shutting down the computer. Paige frowned as she studied the screen for a few moments. She had finished her work assignments for the day. It was the first time she had been alone in the flat with some free time on her hands. She furtively glanced toward the door as if to confirm that she was truly alone, then called up the files containing the public relations and marketing material about all Bryce's companies that he had mentioned the first night. She wanted to find out the kind of information he had on her father's company. If he was actively promoting Franklin Industries, then there was a good chance that he intended to keep it in operation which meant the employees' jobs would be secure.

She searched through an impressive list of businesses, but found only a mention of Franklin Industries with no further information. A jab of disappointment surged through her. She didn't know whether to be hurt or angry. She tried to put some logic to it. There wasn't any notation about the company being due for liquidation or any financial reviews. Maybe it was something he hadn't gotten to yet? He had apparently been very involved in putting together the four London projects that they were now finalizing, something that must have taken all his attention.

Paige printed out all the information on the other companies. It was the type of thing that would be put into a brochure, nothing privileged or secret. Was her worst fear a reality? Had he bought Franklin Industries at bottom dollar only to liquidate what he could and then close it down?

But what about the employees? The people who depended on that job to support their families? What would happen to them? Did he plan to simply fire them?

Hurt and anger welled inside her—and a considerable amount of bewilderment. Before meeting him, she did not doubt that conclusion. But now…he was so different from the way she had pictured him. Surely someone who could show so much compassion for one Italian family faced with the loss of their restaurant could not be so ruthless and greedy that he would close down an entire company without regard to the employees. She sat and stared at the screen. The pieces simply did not fit together, some of the puzzle was missing. There had to be some way to find out what he intended to do with her father's company.

Paige started a search through the computer's stored information, looking for anything having to do with Franklin Industries. She found some basic accounting records, but not much more than what had been available to her upon her father's death. The company was broke and without the infusion of new capital it would have been doomed—new capital that her father had believed was coming from Bryce Lexington.

She glanced at the clock. Bryce would be back any minute. She didn't want him to catch her doing an in-depth search through his files, looking through things that had no relationship to her specific job functions or their business trip to London. She quickly shut the computer down and left the office just as he came in the front door.

"You're back already. That was a quick trip." She offered him a pleasant smile, even if it was a somewhat guilty one.

Her slightly flustered demeanor did not escape Bryce's attention. What had she been up to that made her look and act so guilty? He didn't allow any hint of his thoughts as he returned her smile. "I was lucky, there wasn't much of a line at the box office and there were still some good seats for tonight's performance." He held out the tickets toward her.

She took them from his hand and examined them. "These are excellent seats. It's surprising they were still available at the last minute like this."

"Let's have dinner at Antonio's restaurant after the theater. We'll fly back to Los Angeles first thing in the morning."

A warm glow of contentment settled deep inside her. Their gazes remained locked for a brief moment, then embarrassment caused her to turn away. "I…if you'll excuse me, I'd better start getting ready. I also have packing to do." She went to her room, gathered a few things, then went to the bathroom.

As soon as he heard the shower running he turned his attention to the computer. He quickly logged into a special program he had written and studied the information on the screen. *Hmm…she's been into every file associated with her father's company. I wonder exactly what she's looking for?* A frown wrinkled his forehead for a moment. Was it possible that she didn't know what had happened? That she didn't know what kind of man her father really was? Could her appearance in his life merely be her way of searching for answers? It was a puzzle.

He stared at the screen for a moment longer, his mind lost in thought. Again he battled internally over his decision to go along with her charade until it had played out to her satisfaction—until she had gotten what she wanted. In his heart he truly believed that Paige was not a threat to him, but he needed to be thinking with his head rather than his emotions and that part of him was not sure what was happening. He finally shut down the computer and changed clothes to go to the theater.

The play was everything the critics claimed. Paige enjoyed it immensely. Following the play they took a taxi to Antonio's. During the ride they discussed the play and the various aspects each had particularly enjoyed.

Antonio greeted Paige and Bryce warmly, immediately ushering them to a quiet table. As before, the food was excellent and the service exceptional. Rudy was their waiter and Angela stopped by their table to say hello. They didn't have the luxury of lingering over their meal due to the lateness of the hour.

As Bryce paid the bill, Antonio leaned over to Paige and whispered in her ear, "He's all business, this one—he works too hard. He needs someone just like you. He doesn't think he needs anyone, but I see the way he looks at you. He doesn't fool these old eyes. You take good care of my friend. He's a very special man." He gave a pat and squeeze to her hand followed by a quick wink.

Before Paige could respond to Antonio's words and gesture, Bryce was at her side. "Come on, Bradford. We've got packing to do." He quickly steered her out of the restaurant and into the crisp night air. They walked the short distance back to the flat.

An awkward silence filled the air. Neither wanted to part from the other but there was no logical reason to linger in the living room. Bryce felt particularly ill-at-ease about what could have been considered improper advances that he had already made toward her, particularly if Joe Thompkins was right about her ulterior motives.

In spite of the possibly dire consequences, he wanted very much to enfold her in his arms—to hold her and again taste the sweetness of her kiss and feel the softness of her lips.

They stood in the hallway. "Well…" Her voice was tinged with just a hint of reluctance. "It's getting late. I'd better finish my packing." Antonio's words remained in her consciousness, his contention that Bryce needed her and was obviously interested. She made no effort to turn toward her room.

"Yes," his voice contained the same reluctance, "I'd better get busy, too." He also made no effort to move. He tentatively reached out and took her hand in his, his eyes searching hers for any hint of her feelings, some clue as to what would be proper and acceptable. "When we get back to Los Angeles…would you…I'd like it very much if we could have dinner together sometime."

"We just had dinner together." Paige's words were barely above a whisper. His hand grasped hers, sending a warm feeling up her arm and through her body.

"I meant a non–tax deductible dinner, something strictly social without any hint of business."

"Are you asking me for a date?" All the air seemed to have been sucked from the room and Paige felt as if the furnace had kicked into high gear. She was acutely aware that not only was Bryce still holding her hand, he had slowly laced their fingers together.

"Yes, that's exactly what I'm doing…on one condition." He decided to express his concerns in a straightforward and honest way, in the manner he preferred to do everything.

"One condition?" She could barely get out the words. "What would that be?"

"The condition—" he plumbed the depths of her eyes, almost as if he were searching for something "—is that you are able to clearly separate business from social. I don't want you to feel pressured by any feeling that this is something expected of you—that it's part of your job. If you don't want to accept a date with me, then just say so. It won't have any bearing on your job or our work situation.''

Bryce still was not sure about whether or not Paige felt pressured, but he consoled himself with the thought that if she was after something sinister she would not hesitate to jump in bed with him. In fact, she would probably have been the aggressor their first night in London. He waited for her answer, almost afraid to breathe.

Paige felt the unmistakable pull of his magnetism, felt herself being drawn in tighter and tighter until there was no room left. She recalled their first kiss on the terrace of the French embassy. It had not been much more than a fleeting brushing of their lips, but it had left her wanting much more. Then there was the longer kiss and the way he had suddenly broken away from her and sent her to her room as if she was a child who had misbehaved.

What was happening between them had to be wrong. How could she allow a personal relationship when there were still so many unanswered questions about her father's suicide and about Bryce Lexington's complicity? She was moving farther and farther from her original goal of proving his responsibility in her father's downfall. However, at that moment she would have gladly accepted the fact that there was nothing hidden away for her to pursue...other than Bryce Lexington himself.

She knew she wasn't speaking, yet it was her voice she heard saying the words. "I would like very much to have dinner with you, strictly social and not business."

As they talked and stared into each other's eyes, he slowly and steadily pulled her toward him until he was able to bend his head and capture her mouth with his. He moved their clasped hands behind her back and held her body to his.

A sultry seduction—as much emotional as physical—was taking place. His kiss deepened until the heat of his desires, matched spark for spark by her own desires, almost exploded into flames.

Paige's mind whirled. Never had she experienced such an incendiary explosion of unbridled passion from just one kiss. She had not allowed herself any personal involvement since her divorce, certainly not physical. Nor had she placed trust in anyone since then, especially not emotional trust. It had been too long and Bryce was much too tempting. It was more than her physical passions and needs that he aroused. He burned right through to the depth of her soul. She knew she should be putting a stop to this, but she was not quite ready for the moment to end. She wanted to savor the delicious ecstasy just a little longer.

Paige trembled in his arms. Bryce felt her passionate response to his kiss. He had recognized the danger the first night they were in London, when he had checked in on her as she slept. She was an addictive combination of brains, beauty and independence. And now he could add to that list a sensuality that could wake the dead.

Propriety be damned. Joe Thompkins's warnings be damned. He did not want this to stop. He seductively twined his tongue with hers, tasting the dark recesses of her sweet mouth. Somehow he had to sort things out. He wanted everything—he wanted it all. Was that asking too much? Was this the one thing that the man who seemed to have everything would find too elusive?

The private jet taxied down the runway, then lifted off headed westward back to Los Angeles.

It had been a very shaken Paige who, the night before,

had reluctantly broken off the kiss and silently turned and went inside her room. She knew that if things had continued as they were that both of them would have ended up in the same bed. Not that it would have been an unwanted result of momentary passion. Quite the contrary. At that very moment there had been nothing she wanted more than for Bryce Lexington to make love to her even though the entire situation was in violation of all her stated goals.

She was as perplexed about him as she was about the role he played in her father's demise, about the desires and longings he stirred in her and whether or not she could trust him with her feelings. If only she knew the truth, then she could feel more comfortable about what had transpired between them and what was obviously turning into a personal relationship, a very personal relationship—at least on her part. Several hours had passed before she had finally fallen asleep. His kiss and the heated passion that sizzled between them had lingered with her long after she had gone to bed, causing her to toss and turn until exhaustion had finally claimed her.

Bryce had not slipped into a peaceful sleep either. He had admitted to himself that Paige had been right to break it off. It had been the most expedient thing to do, but he had been unable to bring himself to break it off as he had previously done, to willingly give up the delicious taste and texture of her mouth.

Things had been decidedly awkward that morning when each had emerged from their separate rooms. Bryce had felt he needed to apologize, but did not have a clue as to how to go about it or exactly what he needed to apologize for. Paige, on the other hand, had felt the need to convince him that she did not fall into the arms of every man she came in contact with, especially one she had just met.

It was Bryce who had finally broken the ice, gotten them

past the point of polite *good morning* and *did you sleep well*. He poured each of them a cup of coffee and handed one of the mugs to her. "How about having our dinner date the day after tomorrow? That will be two days before we leave for Aspen."

Her smile was shy, but engaging. "That will be fine." She was very pleased that he had mentioned it. She was afraid he might have forgotten about the date, or had not been serious about it in the first place.

The jet touched down and they quickly cleared customs. Before he put her into her car to send her home, he confirmed the next day's work schedule. "This, Bradford—" he handed her a piece of paper "—is my home address. We'll be working at my house for the next four days. Be there at seven o'clock tomorrow morning. I like to get an early start." With that, he disappeared back inside the hangar.

She was not quite sure what it meant. He seemed to be all business again. Was it merely the remembrance of the glittery reception at the embassy, the evening at the theater, the excitement of London, the good dinner and fine wine that had prompted him to ask her for the date? Even though he had just confirmed the date, did he now regret having become momentarily involved on a personal level? Was this his way of detaching himself from the personal and putting the situation back on a solid business footing? He was a very complex man and becoming more so with each passing day.

Paige found jet lag easier to deal with when traveling from Europe back to the States. She decided to stay awake the rest of the afternoon, then go to bed early that evening to readjust herself to the Los Angeles time schedule. The next four days sounded as if they were going to be very hectic, then they would be leaving for Aspen. She unpacked and did her laundry.

Paige was about to close her closet door when she paused and stared at the clothes hanging there. The evening gown she had worn to the embassy reception glittered on its hanger. She had offered to pay for it, but Bryce had refused to take the money. She reached out and slowly ran her fingers over the soft fabric of the skirt, then touched the sparkling beads that covered the bodice. She closed her eyes and visualized that night—the bright moonlight bathing the beautiful gardens in a silvery glow, Bryce holding her in his arms as they moved to the soft strains of the dance music.

She felt a warm flush come to her cheeks and the back of her neck. Paige realized that moment when Bryce had taken her into his arms was the exact moment she had started falling in love with him. It defied all manner of logic and rationale. But she knew it as surely as she knew that her love would never be returned.

A man like Bryce would require a very special type of woman, someone who could be his equal—someone as dynamic as he was. She was sure he was the type of man who would never be happy with a helpless clinging vine who looked up at him like an adoring puppy, someone who would be merely decorative. He would want someone assertive and confident. She wondered if she had that type of confidence and inner strength. Did she have even a slight chance of winning his heart? Were the occasions when he had kissed her the result of true emotion on his part or merely physical desire prompted by circumstance?

She shook the thoughts from her head. None of this was real. She could not possibly be falling in love with the man who somehow figured in her father's suicide. She forced her thoughts back to the situation at hand. Skiing—he said they would be going skiing while in Aspen. What had she done with her ski clothes? It was difficult to think about skiing with the Los Angeles temperature in the seventies and the sun shining brightly. It was the kind of day that made you think of the beach, not snow. It had been a couple of years since she had been on the slopes. She hoped she would not embarrass him too much with her barely adequate skills.

She finally located her ski clothes and set them out to go to the dry cleaners. She sorted through the accumulated mail she had picked up at the post office on her way home from the hangar. After stifling a yawn, she checked the freezer for something she could pop into the microwave for dinner. It had been a long day and she was very tired.

Following a good night's sleep Paige woke feeling rested. She hurried to prepare for the workday at Bryce's house, not sure exactly what to expect.

At precisely seven o'clock she pulled her car into the circular parking area in front of the house. It was a large Spanish-style home with a red tile roof perched in stately grandeur on the top of a hill overlooking Santa Monica Bay. The front gates stood open revealing the long curved driveway that led from the street up to the house. The grounds were nicely landscaped, the lawn perfectly manicured. A profusion of bright spring colors lined the driveway and blanketed the flower beds along the front of the house.

The wooden double doors with the beveled-glass oval window inserts swung open as she walked up the front steps of the porch. "Good morning, Bradford. You're right on time."

He looked gorgeous standing there in front of her with a towel slung around his neck, wearing a wet swimsuit and nothing else. His tousled hair was damp and had been loosely towel dried. It appeared that he had just come from the pool. His nearness caused tremors of excitement to course through her. It was the same type of sensual excitement she felt in London when he stood framed in the office door dripping wet from the shower and wearing only a towel wrapped around his hips, the same type of excitement she felt when he held her in his arms as they moved to the music on the terrace of the embassy. It was also the same type of excitement she felt the first time his lips had touched hers.

Paige quickly regained her composure even though she suspected her cheeks were bright red with embarrassment. "You startled me." Having him open the door personally and before she even rang the doorbell caught her off guard. She had assumed a servant would answer. "I was expecting—"

"Startled you? This is where you're supposed to be, isn't it? Weren't you expecting someone to open the door for you?"

"Not before I rang the doorbell."

Bryce stepped aside, motioning for Paige to come in. She looked fresh, rested and utterly delicious. It caused a momentary lapse before he regained control of his emotions. He caught just a hint of her perfume as she walked past him. She was dressed in a pair of crisp white slacks topped by a bright orange short-sleeved pullover cotton shirt. She wore orange leather sandals on her bare feet. Her hair was loosely pulled back at the nape.

"Besides, I assumed you'd have a—"

"A what, Bradford?" Bryce strode through the foyer and toward the back of the house. Paige had to almost run to keep up with his fast, long-legged pace.

"A servant—a housekeeper or something."

He abruptly stopped and turned toward her, causing her

to literally run into him. He quickly grabbed her shoulders to prevent her from falling. "Or something?" A slight grin played at the corners of his mouth. "Maybe a butler in striped pants and tails?" Instead of turning her loose, he pulled her closer to him. His voice was soft, his breath tickling her cheek. "I'm capable of opening a door by myself."

He held her a moment longer, inhaling the delicate fragrance of her perfume while studying the wariness in her eyes. "In answer to your question—" he brushed a loose tendril of hair away from her face, allowing his fingertips to linger just a moment on her cheek before releasing her from his grasp "—I do have a housekeeper. She comes in three times a week."

Bryce's nearness was intoxicating. Paige took a step backward and finally managed to stammer, "This is a very lovely house." It was the same as his jet—he tended to things himself rather than hiring someone to wait on him.

"Thank you. Let me take you on a tour before we go out to the office complex."

She had expected the house and its furnishings to be contemporary. She half expected to see the art collection she had assumed he owned. Once again, he surprised her, his home not fitting into her preconceived notions. It was a large, old two-story white Spanish house with graceful archways and a red tile roof. It was furnished with an eclectic mixture of antiques and contemporary. It looked like something that would have graced the cover of *Architectural Digest* magazine.

The ground floor consisted of a formal living room and dining room, a library, a den, a gourmet kitchen with breakfast nook and a very large informal entertainment room that opened onto the patio and pool area. He showed her the downstairs and only mentioned in passing that the upstairs contained bedrooms and bathrooms—four guest rooms and a large master suite. There were servants' quarters in a separate apartment above the three-car garage, but no one used them.

Bryce escorted her outdoors to the pool. The bright sunlight assured another beautiful, warm day. She paused as she took in the scene. The backyard was very large, Paige could not even guess how much land surrounded the house. Beyond the pool was a tennis court. There were two pool houses. He explained to her that one of them was his home office complex and the other was used for pool parties, giving guests a place to change into their swimsuits, and a small kitchen for preparing snacks. Next to the pool, at the edge of the patio, was a hot tub. There did not seem to be anything missing from this perfect environment for entertaining either business associates or friends. Every bit of it was done with impeccable taste and a real flair for style.

"Did you decorate all of this yourself?"

"Some of it. The rest was done by a professional decorator under my direction." Bryce studied her. He could not help wondering if this was the type of home where she would feel comfortable, the type of house she would want to live in. His question was almost hesitant, his voice conveying a tentative quality that people who knew him would never associate with Bryce Lexington. "Do you like it?"

Paige allowed a soft smile to turn the corners of her mouth, her words contained the same softness. "Yes, I do. I like it very much." She could not stop herself from wondering what it would be like to live in such a magnificent house surrounded by all these beautiful things. But it wouldn't matter if she lived in a hovel as long as it was with Bryce. She managed to shove *that* thought away as soon as it crystallized in her consciousness.

"Come on, Bradford. We've work to do." Bryce quickly

brought Paige's mind back to the reality of the day's business. He steered her out the door and across the patio toward the office complex. "This is the nerve center, even more so than the corporate offices I maintain. This is where everything originates."

She looked around. The office complex consisted of a kitchenette, a bathroom and two other rooms—what would normally have been a living room and a bedroom. The living room functioned as the main office with the computer, fax machine, copy machine and a couple of desks and a small table with four chairs. The bedroom was a small private office with a desk and another computer terminal. There was a phone system with four incoming lines that she assumed were different from the phones in the main house.

Paige eyed the computer. If this was his main place of business, then perhaps she could find more information about her father's company. It might be connected to a mainframe at his corporate headquarters where there would be more detailed information stored than what was available in London. She hoped she would have a chance during the next four days to go through the computer files and check them out before they left for Aspen.

"There's coffee already made in the kitchen. I'll be right back." He went to the main house, then returned to the office fifteen minutes later dressed in jeans and a T-shirt. She was relieved that he had changed out of his swimsuit. She was not sure exactly how she would have been able to concentrate on what needed to be done with this gorgeous, half-naked man in such proximity.

They immediately got to work. Bryce explained the basics of three new projects he was interested in developing, projects in the very early planning stages. His turquoise eyes sparkled with excitement as he told her what he hoped to accomplish. It was a real education just listening to the way his mind worked as he outlined specific details, the way he latched onto one small bit of information, expanded upon it, then projected it forward and showed her how it fit into his ultimate goal for that particular project. His enthusiasm was contagious as he made things come to life. The sensation was similar to being swept up in a tornado, the magnitude of his energy almost too much to fully comprehend.

They had stopped briefly about noon, just long enough to grab a sandwich for lunch, then they had gone right back to work. It was almost three o'clock by the time Bryce finished going over the new projects. He shoved the file folders in the desk drawer, indicating that he was finished. "Come on, Bradford. Let's go for a swim, then call it a day."

"Swim?" Her surprise was evident in the startled expression on her face and the tone in her voice.

He frowned as he stared at her for a moment. "You do know how to swim, don't you?"

"Yes, of course. But I didn't bring a swimsuit with me. It never occurred to me that I should and you didn't say anything about it."

"Check out the pool house. There are lots of clean swimsuits in there. I'm sure there's something that will fit you." He paused for a moment as he slowly circled her, his gaze lingering just a little longer on a curve here and another curve there. "In fact, I'm positive there's a suit that will fit you perfectly. It's the red one. You go change while I hang the Closed for the Day sign on the office door and change into my swimsuit."

Bryce went to the main house and she went to the pool house. She could not resist shaking her head. She still did not know what to make of him. Every time she thought she had him figured out, he did something entirely different from what she had anticipated. She found the red swimsuit, what there was of it, and out of curiosity tried it on.

Paige looked at herself in the full-length mirror. He had been correct. The red suit fit her perfectly although there wasn't much to it. She was certainly no prude, far from it. Her own swimsuit was a two-piece suit, but this did not have enough material in it to—

"Bradford! Are you going to spend all day in there?" His voice came from just the other side of the closed door.

"Uh…no, of course not. It's just that this suit—"

"What's the matter, doesn't it fit?"

"Well, yes. It fits…sort of."

"What do you mean, *sort of?* Are you dressed or not? If not, you'd better say so because I'm coming in." Hearing no response, Bryce turned the handle and pulled the door open. He took one step forward, then stopped dead in his tracks. There was nothing subtle about the rapid increase of his pulse rate. He had never seen anyone look so wildly, deliciously sexy and at the same time so properly demure. It was an incredibly stimulating combination. He tried to speak, but no words came out.

Six

The look on Bryce Lexington's handsome face said it all. He liked what he saw, liked it very much. Paige felt an inexplicable tingle of excitement as he continued to stare at her. She imagined it must be akin to the type of thrill an exhibitionist felt. Just a few moments, however, was all the thrill lasted before embarrassment overcame her and she reached for a beach jacket. She quickly pulled it on, covering her body from shoulders to midthigh. "I've never worn such a skimpy—"

"Tomorrow, Bradford..." Bryce paused to take a calming breath and slow down his words, "tomorrow bring your own swimsuit." He quickly turned and left the pool house without even pausing to look back. He executed a running dive into the pool and began swimming laps as if he were in competition for the Olympic gold. He did not know what else to do. It took every fiber of willpower to keep from pulling her into his arms, carrying her off to the bedroom and spending the entire night making love to her slowly, passionately, deliciously and totally.

He wanted to savor every centimeter of her body, know every place that excited her, lose himself completely to the sensation of every shared intimacy. Almost as much as he wanted to make love to her he wanted to know what she was doing in his life, what she was searching for. He continued to swim until the refreshing feel of the water and the vigorous exercise finally took their toll on his heated desires.

As soon as Bryce dived into the water, Paige closed the door to the pool house. She quickly removed the red thong swimsuit and slipped into another suit, a two-piece suit that was far less revealing. After bringing the thump-thump of her pounding heart back to normal, she went out to the decking. She watched him for a few minutes. His swimming stroke was smooth and powerful, his muscles rippled as his tanned body cut back and forth through the sparkling water seemingly oblivious to her presence.

The sun felt good on her skin as she stretched out on one of the lounge chairs, its warmth soothing her slightly shattered sense of propriety. She closed her eyes. The look of smoldering intensity that Bryce had greeted her with in the pool house popped back into her mind. A tremor of sensual desire made its way through her body, then settled low inside her. Once again she relived every moment of the heated kiss they had shared in London following their evening at the theater.

The choices she had made that brought her to where she was at that moment seemed as if they had come from some bizarre tortured place. She was not sure what she wanted anymore or why she was still there. She probably should have resigned immediately upon their return from London as she had originally planned, but now it was too late. She couldn't dismiss her feelings and desires where Bryce Lexington was concerned. Paige tried to make his image leave her mind, but it refused to vanish.

She did not know how long she had lain on the chaise lounge when suddenly a shadow blocked the warming rays of the sun. She opened her eyes. Bryce stood next to her, looming above as he gazed down at her. Rivulets of water made their way over his taut body, his tanned skin glistened in the late-afternoon sun. He ran his fingers through his wet hair to smooth it back out of his eyes. "The water's perfect, Bradford. Why don't you come on in?"

Before she could answer, Bryce impulsively scooped her up in his arms and quickly carried her to the edge of the pool. He held her out precariously over the water. "This is it, Bradford. Sink or swim time."

Her eyes widened in surprise, then she began to laugh as she instinctively grabbed him tightly around the neck to keep from falling. "You wouldn't dare!"

He laughed with her. "Unless you can come up with a good reason why not in the next five seconds that's exactly what I intend to do." He swung her out over the water, then brought her back, each time counting off the seconds. "One…two…three…" Then it happened. She was prepared for the count of five, but not three. Without warning he jumped into the deep end of the pool with Paige still in his arms.

He continued to hold on to her and she continued to cling to him as they sank under the water. He pushed off from the bottom of the pool and they quickly rose toward the surface. They exploded through the top of the water into the air, both laughing at the game with the carefree abandon of children at play.

Paige sputtered through a mouthful of water and an almost uncontrollable laughter. "Not fair! You told me I had until the count of five!"

He continued to hold her as he made his way to the edge of the pool. His voice teased, "What's the matter? Haven't you ever heard the expression *all's fair in love and war?*" The words had slipped out of his mouth before he could stop them. He backed her up against the side of the pool, his body pressing against hers. He looked into the depths of her eyes, not exactly sure how to interpret what he saw. He hoped it was the same intense longing and desire he felt, the same burning passion, but he wasn't sure. Bryce Lexington, a man who could read people like a book, still found her to be an enigma.

He smoothed back her wet hair, then cupped her chin in his hand. His words were soft, as soft as the manner in which he brushed his lips against hers. "Perhaps a better question might be which one of those two choices is this? It's a question that I don't think has an answer, at least not yet." Those may have been his words, but his thoughts told him that the answer he wanted to avoid was perilously close at hand.

She wanted to say something. She wanted to tell him that as far as she was concerned the question had a very definite answer. It was love, no doubt about it. She wanted to say it, but she chose not to. Even if she had been willing to say the words out loud, his mouth was on hers before she could speak.

The water was too deep for her feet to reach the bottom. An instinctive need to be somehow anchored to something solid and safe caused her to wrap her legs around his hips at the same time as she tightened her arms around his neck. He pressed forward, pinning her between the side wall of the pool and his body.

All the passion, all the fire, all the silent promises of

things yet to be were once again transmitted to her through his kiss. His tongue sent intense tremors of excitement coursing through her body as it brushed against hers in a seductive mating ritual. She wanted him. The hardness of his body as his bare skin pressed against hers—she wanted him now. She wanted...

She wanted to get her desires under control before she made a complete fool of herself. The last thing Paige needed was for Bryce to think she was the type of woman who would readily hop into bed with just anyone.

With great difficulty he managed to break off the heated kiss, but continued to press his body against hers. Her sensual warmth was driving him crazy. "Bradford, if we don't stop this right now there's only one place it can lead and I'm not sure you're quite ready to take that big of a step, especially with us knowing each other such a short time." His voice was husky, his words thick with the passion that churned inside him.

His voice had dropped so low she had to strain to hear him. "I'm not sure whether you can truly separate business from personal, that you're not feeling pressured into something you don't want or aren't ready for."

The time for testing and analyzing was over. Paige knew exactly what she wanted. She looked him square in the eye and spoke with as much confidence as she could muster. "You, Bryce Lexington, may be in charge of all you survey and can run a business empire from your head, but there's one thing you can't do because I won't allow it." She paused, noting the concern, disappointment, maybe even a little bit of hurt that darted through the turquoise depths of his eyes. "I won't allow you to make my decisions for me. I'm a big girl. If I want this stopped, then I can say so."

His heart pounded in his chest as the excitement took hold. "So tell me, Paige Bradford..." He pulled her tighter against his body, the water lapping gently around their shoulders. He was almost afraid to ask. "Do you want this stopped?"

This was the moment of truth. Did she dare trust this man? Did she dare give herself to the one person who had been the obsession of her revenge thoughts for six months? The words came out before she had time to stop them.

"Do I want this stopped? No."

Paige's voice became soft, for the first time her concerns and fears showed. She spoke hesitantly, not sure of exactly how to put her thoughts into words. "You must think I'm terribly brazen and aggressive. Please don't think that I willingly submit to just anyone and everyone who—"

Bryce placed his fingertips against her lips to still her words. A warm, loving smile lit up his face as he spoke. "Now you're making my decisions for me, trying to tell me what I should and shouldn't think. Let me tell you exactly what I think. The truth is I think you're the most exciting woman I've ever met and not for one moment do I believe that you're easily seduced." For Bryce, it was quite a revealing statement of his inner thoughts and feelings, far more than he usually exposed of his personal self.

Her heart melted as she looked into his eyes. His words had caught her completely by surprise. Maybe she was seeing what she wanted to, but his eyes showed honesty without a trace of deception. "Me? You think I'm—"

"I think you, Paige Bradford, are incredibly desirable and I want to make love to you right now."

Paige was acutely aware of the way their bodies were entwined and pressed together. Bryce's arms were wrapped around her while he stood on the bottom of the pool with her arms and legs wrapped around him. He moved slowly through the water toward the shallow end, carrying her with him. As he walked, he nuzzled her neck and nibbled on her earlobe, then slowly kissed his way across her cheek toward the corners of her mouth. With one hand he deftly unhooked the back of her swimsuit top. Only the strap tied behind her neck prevented it from falling away.

The cool water rushed inside the loosened top, swirling around her bare breasts and teasing her nipples to taut peaks. She felt a quick jab of pure lust as the fervor of her desire increased severalfold. Were they going to make love right here in the pool? On the deck next to the pool? It all seemed so forbidden...and so very exciting. She had to admit that her intimate relationships, not that there had been that many, had always lacked this type of spontaneity, sensual excitement and sexual heat. The emotions coursing through her almost took her breath away as she gave herself over to them.

His mouth devoured hers, his kiss hot and demanding. Her response was everything he had hoped it would be. She met every one of his unspoken demands with demands of her own. They reached the shallow end of the pool. He continued to hold her and she continued to cling to him, her arms wrapped around his neck. He trailed one hand across her bare back to her rib cage, then slowly cupped the firm flesh of her breast. Her puckered nipple pressed into his palm sent tremors through his body.

The ringing phone shattered the surrounding silence and the sexually charged atmosphere. Bryce lifted Paige up, seated her on the decking at the edge of the pool, buried his face between her breasts, then quickly took one tautly pointed nipple into his mouth. He held it there for only a moment before releasing it. He fought to bring his breathing under control, then expelled a loud breath of irritation. "That's the call I've been expecting from Chicago. Of all the lousy timing."

Paige wiggled out of his grasp and quickly stood up. She

adjusted the top of her swimsuit so that it covered her exposed breasts. She handed him a towel. "I'll answer it while you dry off."

Bryce climbed out of the pool and began drying himself. His gaze never left her retreating form as she walked across the patio and disappeared into the office. He looped the towel around his neck and followed her, reaching the office door just as she stepped back out into the orange glow of the setting sun. He paused long enough to brush his lips against hers, then disappeared inside the office.

It was time to once again become a businessman.

Paige picked at her dinner as she sat in her living room in front of the television trying to concentrate on the evening news. While Bryce took care of his call from Chicago she had changed back into her own clothes. The mood had been broken. For them to have made love after he finished with his phone call would have seemed too calculating, somehow planned and scheduled. The spontaneity of the moment had come and gone.

She was not sure whether she was relieved or disappointed by the turn of events. Perhaps fate had stepped in and saved her from making a horrible mistake, from doing something she would end up regretting. Thoughts about her father tried to formulate, but she refused to allow them to reach maturity. It seemed that her father's dealings with Bryce and the ruination of Franklin Industries had steadily dropped from her prime concern to a distant secondary consideration. She desperately needed to get her priorities straightened out.

It was no longer so much a matter of proving Bryce's culpability in her father's suicide as it was trying to figure out what had happened between Bryce and her father. The welfare of her father's employees was still of great concern to her, but of equal concern was her fear that she might once again be putting her trust in a man who was only deceiving her. But didn't love and trust go hand in hand? Could there be love without trust?

Things were becoming very complicated. Her dedication to her cause had slowly been eroded by the intensity of her own desires and her feelings about Bryce. Paige toyed with her fork, pushing the green beans around the plate and jabbing at a tomato wedge. Finally she dropped the fork and shoved the plate away, allowing a sigh to escape her lips. Why did life have to be so difficult? She tried watching television, but found nothing of interest. She finally grabbed a book and went to bed.

Bryce stood in his kitchen in front of the opened refrigerator door and stared at the contents. He finally reached for something even though nothing really sparked his taste buds.

There had been no surprise when he emerged from the inner office following his phone call and found Paige dressed in her regular clothes. The call had broken the mood. As much as he wanted to pick up the seduction where they had left off, he knew the time was now all wrong. He still was concerned that she felt pressured in spite of her words to the contrary.

And those concerns extended to an uneasiness about the nature of their business relationship. He had never before made any attempt to seek out a personal or intimate relationship with any of his female employees. Joe Thompkins's warnings about her motives still lingered in the back of his mind. He knew he was playing with fire by leaving himself and his company open to the possibility of a sexual harassment suit. He tried to rationalize things by reminding himself that it was she who had invaded his privacy by prying into his personal life. She was there under false pretenses and his sole purpose in having transferred her to his personal staff was to keep an eye on her activities and make sure she didn't do anything that could compromise his business.

His thoughts turned to their date for the following evening. He planned to take her to his favorite restaurant in Newport Beach. He wanted the evening to be very special. Picking her up at her apartment for a date would put the evening on a personal level, dissociate it from business. Bryce climbed the stairs to the second floor after grabbing a book from the library.

He read for a while, then finally fell asleep.

The next morning promptly at seven o'clock he heard the doorbell ring. He opened the front door. "Come on, Bradford. We have lots to do." He headed immediately back to the office. Bryce had already made coffee and had been working for an hour prior to Paige's arrival. She had been a little anxious about the possibility of a strained atmosphere surrounding their working relationship after what had happened the previous afternoon, but just as it had been in London, she soon realized she had no reason to worry. He was all business, yet things were comfortable and cordial. She did not feel even a hint of any awkwardness or a strained situation.

There was work to be done and that was what they did, leaving the personal aspects of their developing relationship for another time. As Paige watched him she began to understand his separation of business and personal. They worked straight through for the entire day, eating lunch while they continued to work. Most of their time and efforts were directed to the new project connected with his phone call from Chicago.

At four o'clock Bryce walked over to her desk and stood

behind her as she finished revising one of the computer files. As soon as she completed the computer functions, he reached past her and shut down the machine.

His action startled her. She had been aware of him standing behind her, but had been absorbed in her work. Paige quickly spun around in her chair and looked questioningly at him. "I still have more to do." She placed her hand on top of a stack of file folders. "Look at all this. Why did you turn off the computer?"

His eyes sparkled as a dazzling smile covered his face. "The rest of this can wait until tomorrow." He took her hand in his and pulled her up out of the chair. "We have a date tonight." The smile faded as he looked into her eyes. He ran his fingertips lightly across the smooth skin of her cheek, then brushed her hair away from her face. "Remember?"

Her breathing quickened and her insides trembled in response to his touch. "Yes, I remember."

He cupped her face in his hands. "Why don't you leave now. I'll pick you up at six-thirty. Will that give you enough time to get ready?"

She automatically reached her hands up and placed them on top of his, her voice almost a whisper. "Yes, that will be plenty of time." Paige hurried home to get ready for her date.

*Date...*the word had an odd sound and feel to it. So far their relationship had been a strange mixture of hard work and searing desire, the two dynamics connected yet kept in their own separate little compartments. A little tremor of anxiety rippled through her. What would the night bring?

She showered, applied her makeup, then put on a blue knee-length chiffon cocktail dress. She frowned as she stared at herself in the mirror. Was she overdressed? What if he was wearing jeans? The doorbell rang, cutting off any further speculation. She opened the door to an incredibly handsome man looking every bit the dynamic and powerful executive he was. They drove to Newport Beach in time for their dinner reservation.

Paige and Bryce were seated in a quiet corner of a very elegant restaurant with a view looking out over the water. Millions of sparkling city lights lined the bay. The table was covered with a fine linen cloth and set with crystal, china and sterling. Subdued candlelight flickered seductively and a small arrangement of bright spring flowers added a dash of color. Soft music played in the background.

He looked so very handsome in his tailored charcoal-gray suit. Paige was sure every woman in the restaurant was secretly lusting after him and looking at their own dinner companions with a sense of disappointment. The aroma of his aftershave sent little shivers down her spine.

Their dinner conversation flowed comfortably. The mood was soft and very sensual. The glow of the candlelight enhanced the warm glow created by the champagne…a glow that was slowly, but steadily, heating up the passions that each of them knew could flare into an explosion of desire with very little effort. They lingered over their after-dinner coffee. The entire time that they talked Bryce ran his fingertips across the back of Paige's hand, covered her hand with his and occasionally laced their fingers together for a few moments at a time.

"Would you like anything else? Maybe some dessert?" His voice was soft, almost a caress as he captured her look and held it.

"No. Dinner was delicious, but I couldn't eat another bite." Her heart beat a little faster in anticipation of the rest of the evening.

The heated moment remained suspended in the air between them. Without further conversation, he rose from his chair and held hers as she stood. He took her hand in his and they exited the restaurant. Traffic was light, it would only take about forty-five minutes for the drive from Newport Beach to Santa Monica.

Paige rested her head back against the car seat with her eyes closed, a contented smile curling the corners of her mouth. It had been a marvelous dinner, everything had been absolutely perfect and the most perfect thing about the entire evening had been Bryce. Each passing minute pulled her farther and farther into the magnetic whirl of this very dynamic man. A brief thought about how she had become involved with him to begin with tried to penetrate the sensual cloud that surrounded her reality, but without success.

They drove along in silence for several minutes, each seemingly content with the warmth of the moment. Bryce glanced over at her as he drove north along the freeway, the dim light from the dashboard offering just enough illumination to highlight her finely sculpted features. She was everything he had been searching for, everything he would ever need, everything he could ever want. He reached over and clasped her hand in his. But he could not escape the nagging question in the back of his mind that kept asking why she had invaded his life and what she wanted.

He dismissed the bothersome thoughts from his mind. "I have a very old bottle of cognac at my house that's just been waiting for a special occasion. I think tonight has been that occasion and I'd like to share the cognac with the person who made it so special."

"Thank you." His words sent a sensual warmth flowing through her body until it touched every part of her. She couldn't have refused his invitation even if she wanted to.

Twenty minutes later they arrived at Bryce's house. He led Paige into the library. It was a cozy room with a wood-burning fireplace. He removed his suit jacket and draped it across the back of a chair. He paused a moment to loosen his tie and unfasten the top button on his shirt before lighting the fire. He closed the glass fireplace doors, then turned off the table lamp. The flames provided the only illumination. The seductive dance of shadow and light played across the walls enhancing the already highly charged atmosphere that surrounded them. He turned on the stereo. The soft music playing in the background enhanced the setting.

Bryce produced the bottle of cognac and poured two glasses, handing one of them to Paige. They sat on the couch sipping their drinks. The mood was soft and very sensual. A tingle of sexual electricity filled the air. The magnetic pull tugging at them could not in any way be called subtle.

His turquoise eyes burned with his desires. She felt the heat as surely as if she had placed her hand on one of the burning logs in the fireplace. As soon as he suggested they go to his house to share an after-dinner cognac she knew they would make love. She also knew that Bryce would be a very exciting lover. He had already touched the depths of her soul with an intriguing mixture of soft tenderness combined with the incendiary fervor of his passions. She loved him. She did not want it to be true, but the fact remained that it was true. She only hoped this wasn't a colossal mistake, that she had not misplaced her trust once again where men were concerned.

He leaned his face into hers, their lips met, their tongues meshed, then the heated passions that had been simmering just below the surface exploded with a force that shocked each of them—a force that barely clung to the constraints of order and control.

No words were spoken as he rose from the couch, pulling

her up with him. She stood in her stocking feet, her shoes resting on the floor next to the couch. He held her body close in his embrace. Her head rested on his chest and his cheek pressed against the top of her hair. He took a calming breath, trying to settle the wild surges of desire coursing through his veins. His voice was husky, his words a tentative whisper. "Paige...are you—"

Her response was as much of a whisper as his unfinished question. "You're not going to ask me if I'm sure about this, are you?"

"No...I guess I'm not." The intimacy of the situation had allowed him to use her first name. He had finally removed the invisible barrier that had kept him at a distance from her, certainly emotionally if not physically. But now the barriers were down. He placed his fingertips under her chin and lifted her face. He peered into the depths of her eyes. He saw his own passion mirrored there. And his pulse raced faster than it already was.

But there was more than the excitement. He became acutely aware of another sensation, too. One that was foreign to him and one that he didn't like. He had never been unsure of himself in any situation. A little tremor of the unfamiliar, a ripple of uncertainty darted through him. He wanted so much to please her, it was very important to him.

He banished his concerns as his mouth came down on hers. A million sensations raced through him all culminating in Paige Bradford—how she felt in his arms, the taste of her mouth...how much he wanted her. But love? It was something he was afraid to face, an area where he feared he would fail. A little tremor of apprehension told him he may have started something that he couldn't control.

Seven

With trembling fingers Bryce lifted the tab of the zipper on the back of Paige's dress and slowly lowered it. The soft fabric slipped off her shoulders, exposing her smooth skin. The scent of her perfume tickled his already stimulated senses. He placed a kiss on her shoulder, then nuzzled the side of her neck as he slowly inched her dress down her arms until it was free to drop to the floor. Her soft moan reached his ears sending a quiver of added anticipation through his body.

He caressed her bare back, reveling in the silky smoothness of her skin. He wanted her more than he had ever wanted anyone in his life. It took a great deal of self-control to keep from giving in to the rush of heated desire by taking her right there on the floor in front of the fireplace, but even more he wanted the sensual expectation to continue. He wanted to spend the entire night making love to her. Then a hard jolt of pure lust hit him as she tugged his shirttail from his slacks. She undid his already loosened necktie and slowly pulled it off, dropping it to the floor. Next her fingers worked at the buttons on the front of his shirt, quickly unfastening them. The growl left his throat as his mouth came down on hers claiming her as his and his alone.

It was unlike her to be so brazen, but Paige didn't seem to have any restraint over her desires or her actions. She readily accepted the sensation of his tongue brushing against hers, the textures meshing and twining in a seductive mating ritual. This man who had been the center of her obsession for the past six months because of his connection to her father's death was now the center of a different reality for her. She ran her hands under his shirt, her fingers trailing across the hard planes of his chest. A multitude of whirling emotions collided inside her, not the least of which was a potent combination of guilt and passion—guilt over allowing herself to become so intimately involved with this man yet a passion more intense than any she had ever before experienced.

She ran her hands inside his open shirt, across his chest and around to his back. She was aware of more than just his mouth on hers. His hands slid across her bare back, every place he touched her skin sending tingles of excitement through her body. He pulled her tighter to him. Her breasts pressed against his bare chest. She could feel his strong heart beat as it resonated to her. She stepped out of the dress that had pooled around her ankles when it dropped to the floor, quickly shoving it aside with her foot.

He slid his hands down her back. When he reached the elastic waist of her panty hose he slipped his hands inside until he was able to cup the roundness of her bottom. His hardened arousal pressed against her when he pulled her hips to his. She let out a soft moan, half submissive and half aggressive.

They stood in the dimly lit library entwined in each other's arms. The soft music settled around them in sharp contrast to the increased urgency of the needs building inside them.

Before she had an opportunity to do or say anything, he pulled off his shirt, dropped it on the floor on top of her dress and scooped her up in his arms. His husky words tickled across her ear. "Let's go upstairs."

Bryce carried her up to his bedroom. She nestled in his arms much as she had the time he carried her through the plane while she slept. Only this time it was different. She was awake and he would not be leaving her there alone. A confusing compilation of thoughts and emotions raced through him. There were so many things he wanted to say to her—and all of them frightened him.

He set her down next to his bed, then allowed his hands to glide across her shoulders and down her arms, finally taking her hands in his. He gave them a little squeeze as he gazed into her eyes. Another nervous tremor tried to occupy his attention, but he refused to succumb to it. He brushed a soft kiss across her mouth. This was not the time and certainly not the place for him to give credence to any doubts.

He released her hands, kicked off his shoes and removed his slacks. A moment later each of them had discarded the last remnants of their clothing. The primal urges that said he wanted everything right now battled with his desire to proceed slowly, to savor each and every intimate moment. He reached out a trembling finger and traced the outline of her delicious mouth. The soft light filtering in from the hallway highlighted the curve of her breasts and enhanced the creamy texture of her skin. No one had ever excited him the way she did. Bryce closed his eyes for a second as he tried to gather his composure.

His excitement radiated to Paige, a rush of sensual fervor that matched her own. He was everything she had ever wanted and far more than what she had hoped for. Yet there were doubts. She knew how she felt about him, but what were his feelings about her? Would her love ever be returned? She banished the negative thoughts when he sank into the softness of the bed, taking her with him. He rolled over so that his body partly covered hers. Her mind filled with new thoughts of what she hoped the future held. But as soon as his mouth came down on hers all thoughts disappeared, leaving only the waves of desire coursing through her body.

His mouth teased, then demanded. She willingly gave him everything he wanted…and more. She tickled her fingers across his tautly muscled back, then allowed her fingertips to trail over the curve of his bottom. The sensation of his hand gliding up her inner thigh infused her with a tremor of delight that moved seductively through her body. She arched her hips upward when his hand reached the moist heat of her femininity, welcoming his intimate touch.

His mouth seemed to be everywhere, his lips nibbling and his tongue teasing—her neck, her throat, her shoulder—finally drawing in her tautly puckered nipple. She ran her fingers through his thick hair, down his rib cage, then reached for his hardened arousal. Her ragged breathing matched his, her wants and needs increasing with each passing moment.

The convulsive waves started deep inside her and quickly spread through her body igniting the last vestige of control that she had been able to hold on to. His lips moved to her other breast, teasing that nipple before taking it into his mouth. She wrapped her fingers around his hardness and felt him shudder in response.

As much as Bryce wanted to prolong the delicious foreplay, he couldn't wait any longer. He reached into the drawer of the nightstand and grabbed the condom packet. A minute later he situated himself between her legs with most of his weight on his elbows, pausing long enough to look into the fiery excitement of her eyes. The smoky sensuality that gazed back at him stole what little control he still possessed. He thrust his hips forward, filling her with his hardness. He sucked in a ragged breath as sensations washed over him, then set a smooth pace.

Her hips rose to meet each of his downstrokes, their bodies moving in harmony as if they were familiar lovers rather than this being their first union. Bryce's mouth came down hard on hers, the incendiary passion existing between them nearly bursting into flame. Their pace escalated, racing toward the ultimate rapture.

Paige tightened her hold on him, her arms and legs wrapped around his body. Her excitement built, expanding layer upon layer until the convulsions ignited inside her in an all-encompassing combination of physical and emotional euphoria stronger than anything she had ever before experienced—a combination she was unable to break down into the two separate components. And out of it floated the word *love*.

Bryce's chest heaved with his labored breathing as he made one final thrust, burying his hardness deep inside her. He held her tightly as the spasms of release spread through his body. Making love had never had such a profound impact on his sensibilities as this had. His physical needs had been met, but there was more than that. There was something very important—something he was afraid to acknowledge. He buried his face in her hair, not sure what to say to her or even exactly what he felt.

He gulped in a lungful of air as he fought to bring his breathing under control. He brushed several loose tendrils of hair away from her damp cheek and forehead, then placed a soft kiss on her lips. He cradled her in his arms, rocking her softly as his mind drifted to thoughts he really didn't want to deal with. He became aware of her slow, even breathing. He placed another kiss on her forehead, then quietly slipped out of bed and headed for the bathroom.

Paige was aware of Bryce leaving the bed, but she remained still as she savored the delights of their lovemaking. He was tender and gentle, yet he had an intensity and passion beyond anything she had ever experienced. The glow of that passion continued to warm her until he returned a couple of minutes later, snuggling his body up against her back. He quickly wrapped his arms around her, cupping the fullness of her breasts in his hands. She placed her hand on his thigh and rubbed her foot against his calf.

Neither of them spoke. Words seemed unnecessary for the time being. She continued to bask in the afterglow of the most exquisite night of her life until sleep finally claimed her thoughts.

Paige didn't know how long she had been sleeping when she gradually opened her eyes and became aware of the daylight filtering in the windows. She stirred, then turned over onto her back. The aroma of fresh coffee tickled her senses. She slowly looked around. She had not paid any attention to the room when she and Bryce had gone upstairs. Her only awareness had been the excitement of Bryce, the way he made her senses race out of control.

It was a very large corner room with windows all along

the two outside walls. A double set of French doors stood open, allowing the fresh air of the sunny morning to enter. The decor, as with the rest of the house, was expensive and in good taste. The room projected a masculine feel yet managed to be soft, warm and comfortable.

"Good morning, or almost afternoon. I was about ready to declare the day a total loss. I've been awake for hours." His voice teased as he reached over and smoothed her mussed hair back from her face. His expression turned serious as he placed a soft kiss on her lips and wrapped her in his embrace. "How do you feel this morning, Paige— are you okay? No regrets or recriminations?"

She closed her eyes and allowed the warmth of his hard body pressed against hers to flow through her consciousness. How did she feel? She felt marvelous, totally head over heels in love. She looked up into the questioning intensity of his eyes noting the slight hint of apprehension and uncertainty hidden there. She extended a warm, happy smile.

"When I first woke I thought for a moment that last night had been only a dream. No…no regrets and no recriminations."

A feeling of relief immediately enveloped him. For the last three hours he had been worried about what her reactions would be when she woke up. He had quietly slipped out of bed and gone down to the pool to swim several laps in an effort to work off the anxiety building layer upon layer inside him. It was an odd feeling, an odd situation. She did things to him, made him think and feel things over which he seemed to have no control. He didn't like the lack of control over his own thoughts and feelings.

He wished he knew why she had been so thoroughly checking him out, what she was looking for, why she had accepted the job without revealing her true identity...why she was here in his bed. Was it all part of some scheme?

He knew he was emotionally involved on a level he had never before experienced, but just how much was a question that truly frightened him, one he didn't want to face. The feeling was compounded by the fact that it all happened so startlingly quick. How did she really feel? What was going on in her head? He held her closer. If only he had the answers to those disturbing questions. And if only his feelings didn't frighten him so much.

Paige, too, was lost in her own thoughts. She pondered what type of woman it would take to capture the heart of someone as dynamic as Bryce Lexington. Did she have any chance at all? She knew he liked her, she could tell that, but how much? More than merely as a lover? Would she be able to secure a permanent place in his heart? A dark thought interrupted her musings. She again thought of her father and the one hundred employees whose jobs and well-being hung in the balance. She needed to know, needed to put that chapter of her life to rest one way or the other before she could get on with her own life.

"Would you like some coffee? I have a fresh pot right here." He indicated the small table by the opened French doors. "We could take it out on the balcony. It's a beautiful day."

"I'd like that." She started to sit up, then wrinkled her forehead into a slight frown as she stared at her panty hose on the floor. "My clothes—"

"I brought a cover-up from the pool house. You could use it as a robe..." An impish gleam flashed through his eyes as he tried to suppress a grin. "Or you could go au naturel. That gets my vote."

She sat upright, holding the blanket in front of her in a shy manner as she slipped her legs over the side of the bed.

"I probably should go home and do something with myself, I must look a mess."

He reached out and took hold of her hand, then pressed it to his lips. "No you don't. You look lovely."

Their gazes locked and a moment later all the heated passion they had shared the night before burst into flame again. He enfolded her into his embrace and brushed his lips softly against hers. "Tomorrow must be a workday, we've lots to do before leaving for Aspen. Today, however..." He nuzzled her neck, then teased her nipple with his tongue until it stood out in a taut peak, "is an officially declared holiday set aside solely for the purpose—" he closed his lips around her puckered nipple and gently suckled for a moment "—of your pleasure." He pulled her down on the bed and seductively ran his hand up her inner thigh. "Now, what would please you?"

Her words came out in a breathless rush. "I think you've found it." Little tremors of anticipation darted across the surface of her skin causing her pulse to race. She wasn't sure where this excitement was going, but she did know that she never wanted it to stop. Each moment of each day Bryce was becoming more and more the center of her universe. She closed her eyes and allowed a contented little smile to curl the corners of her mouth. Once again he propelled her from reality into a sensual world where they shared the heat of their passions.

Another hour passed before they got out of bed, showered and dressed in swimsuits. The rest of the day was spent laughing and playing in the water like kids, enjoying the freedom and openness of the new intimacy of their developing personal relationship.

By late afternoon they sat next to the pool, the warm sun drying out the wet swimsuits they wore. Their lovemaking that morning had, once again, been filled with the excitement of the incendiary desires that enveloped them. There was nothing subtle about the electrically charged atmosphere that sizzled between them.

The long shadows of late afternoon spread across the yard, the air contained the coolness of the approaching evening as the sun dipped low in the sky. They went back to the house so Paige could gather her things and Bryce could drive her home. He had asked her to stay, but knew she was right in her insistence on going home. The next day would be a very busy workday, then the following day they would be flying to Aspen.

He drove her to her apartment, then returned to his house where he fixed himself something to eat. A profound feeling of loneliness settled over him as he wandered around the large house, finally ending up in his bedroom.

Bryce stood on the balcony staring across the yard to the hills beyond as he contemplated what the future held. The word *love* so terrified him that he quickly shoved it aside. He had never been involved in a relationship serious enough for him to allow thoughts of the future of that relationship. But now his head was filled with thoughts of Paige and a future together and even beyond that to the possibility of a family. A renewed sense of hope rose inside him. Perhaps he really would be able to have everything he wanted. The answer rested with Paige. He needed to know what had brought her into his life, what she was after and why.

A quick pang of anxiety stabbed at him. What if he put all of his hopes into this, for the first time exposed his innermost emotions and feelings, allowed someone to see his vulnerability, only to end up hurt, disappointed and rejected? He took in a deep breath, then turned and went back inside.

* * *

"Good morning, Bradford." He stepped aside as she entered the house promptly at seven o'clock the next morning. "We've got a busy day ahead of us." He turned and proceeded through the house to the office structure by the pool.

Considering what had happened between them, it would be logical to expect things to be more intimate, more personal and less businesslike. But she now understood Bryce's concept of separating business from personal and was not offended by his brisk attitude. They had lost an entire day from a busy work schedule and needed to make it up. There would be time later to explore personal feelings.

The day turned out to be even busier than she anticipated. He spent much of the time on the phone trying to bring various facets of his newest project together. The fax machine was in constant use as was the computer. Bryce had made coffee first thing that morning, but it was almost three o'clock, a full eight hours after her arrival, before there was time to stop and think about lunch. They finally took a break and sat out by the pool while grabbing a quick bite to eat. She leaned back in the chair and closed her eyes.

"Tired?" He placed his hands on her shoulders and began to gently massage the kinks from her neck and upper back. He felt her relax as he expertly worked at her tensed muscles. It warmed him to see the contented smile curl the corners of her very tempting mouth.

"Mmm...that feels very good." She continued to lean back with her eyes closed, enjoying his gentle manipulation of her tensed shoulders and neck. His touch revived all the intimate moments they had shared, moments that would be forever burned into her memory. The love she felt for him welled inside her.

"I know it's been a very hectic day, but we accomplished a lot. In fact, we're ahead of schedule. We can devote the time in Aspen entirely to looking at artwork for the London gallery and doing a little skiing and not be bothered by any other business.'' He pulled her hair aside, then leaned forward and brushed his lips against her nape.

She welcomed the personal gesture. It signaled that business was finished for the day. They would be leaving for Aspen in the morning, but in the meantime there was tonight. She took a deep breath, allowing the warmth of his energy to flow through her.

''Let's go for a swim.'' His words tickled in her ear as he leaned closer. ''I know where there's a red swimsuit that looks terrific on you.''

She turned her head toward him, their lips almost touching as she spoke. Her voice was as soft as his had been. ''You don't mean that little wisp of fabric you tried to get me to wear the other day…I might as well have been wearing nothing.''

He flicked his tongue seductively against her lower lip, then reached for her hand, pulling her up out of the chair. His words were wrapped in the heat of his desires. ''That's even better.''

''Bryce!''

His voice teased as he slipped his arms around her. ''There's not a soul around, no one can see us.'' He nuzzled her neck. ''I'll bet you've never been skinny-dipping.'' He captured her mouth with a kiss that began light and teasing, but soon escalated as his passions burst into flame. One hand slid across the delightful roundness of her bottom while he slipped the other up inside the back of her shirt and deftly unhooked her bra. The day's business had definitely come to an end.

She quickly responded to his expert seduction. The mere brushing of his lips against hers set her soul on fire.

* * *

The next day the private jet touched down at the Aspen airport where a rental car waited. Bryce and Paige drove to the house that had been rented for the three days of their stay. It was a beautiful house in a secluded wooded setting, a rustic warmth yet with all the modern amenities.

A large stone fireplace dominated the living room, with thick rugs scattered about on the hardwood floors in a precise manner that was intended to convey casualness. The glass-enclosed deck, containing a hot tub, looked out over the city of Aspen and the surrounding mountains. There was a guest bedroom and a bathroom downstairs. The entire second level consisted of the master suite in a loft with a private bedroom and bathroom and a separate sitting room that overlooked the living room. It, too, had a deck and a fireplace.

The original plan had been for Paige to stay in the guest room downstairs. Now, they would share the master suite in the loft. After unpacking and setting up the laptop computer and portable printer, they were ready to get down to the business at hand.

First on the list was the sculptor. Her studio was two miles away from the house. Paige had been very surprised to find that the sculptor did not carve in marble or model with clay. She worked in metal, primarily bronze. Some of her sculptures were welded, but most of them were cast. It was the type of thing Paige had always considered as a masculine art form rather than being associated with a woman.

The body of the artwork encompassed a wide variety of styles from the new and abstract to the traditional. Paige immediately saw why Bryce was so interested in having this work displayed as part of the London gallery project.

It was dynamic and forceful without being overpowering. Each piece was a unique design lovingly executed.

Next they visited a studio across town to view the watercolor paintings of an up-and-coming young male artist. His work displayed imaginative shapes and designs without compromising traditional values. It was an interesting cross between French impressionist and modern expressionist. His use of color was compelling and original. As with the metal sculpture, this work was certainly worthy of being included in the London gallery.

Bryce was very pleased with both artists and felt their work would be successfully marketed. Details of the contracts were discussed and by the end of the day all negotiations had been completed, everyone satisfied with the outcome. They stopped for dinner, returning to the house after dark.

Bryce put the champagne bottle in the ice bucket, then turned on the hot tub to heat the water to the proper temperature while Paige took care of the computer details concerning the day's business. As soon as she shut down the computer he turned out the lights on the ground level, leaving only the light from the loft to provide the barest of illumination.

"The hot tub is ready, the champagne is ready—" he brushed his lips against hers as he folded her into his embrace "—and I'm ready."

She pressed her body against his, her voice a husky whisper. "So am I."

He took her hand and led her out onto the enclosed deck. Standing next to the hot tub, he cradled her upturned face in his hands and placed a soft, loving kiss on her mouth. He slipped his tongue between her lips, gently probing and exploring the dark recesses of her mouth.

Paige returned his ministrations, twining her tongue with

his and reveling in the texture of his mouth pressed against her. Nothing mattered except Bryce Lexington. Once again the cloudy thoughts concerning her personal business with Bryce about her father's suicide and the fate of the Franklin Industries employees tried to gain entry into her consciousness, but she quickly rejected them. She gave herself wholly to the love she felt for Bryce.

Her softness, her warmth, her responsiveness—she was more than he had ever hoped for, more than he thought was possible. Bryce thought he just might be truly falling in love with her. He knew he would eventually have to take a chance and share those feelings with her, hoping she would return that love. But could he do that before he discovered her hidden agenda? Did he dare venture into that unknown and frightening territory?

He slipped the blouse off her shoulders, allowing it to drop to the floor. He placed a soft kiss on her bare shoulder. Tonight he would be content to lose himself in the soft sensuality of Paige Bradford and eliminate the disturbing thoughts from his mind.

A shiver of sweet anticipation darted across the surface of Paige's skin. Bryce's lips pressed against the side of her neck, nibbled at the juncture of her neck and shoulder, brushed across her cheek. Her hands slipped up under his cashmere sweater and trailed across his hard chest, pausing for a moment to linger on the sensation of his strong heartbeat.

One by one they discarded pieces of their clothing until there was none left. He held her hand and assisted her into the hot tub. The bubbling water swirled around their bodies, adding to the heated sensuality that already filled the air. He opened the champagne and poured two glasses, handing her one of them.

Bryce raised his glass toward her in the form of a toast.

His words were soft, his eyes sparkled with desire. "To a very lovely lady…a lady who is very special to me." They sipped their champagne while looking deeply into each other's eyes. The only sounds were the bubbling of the water and their increased breathing.

He had wanted to say more, but was unable to force the words. He felt his excitement grow and expand as he watched the bubbling water tickle across her breasts, her taut nipples peeking out only to be quickly submerged again.

Paige was thankful for the dim lighting, thankful that he was not able to see the heated flush of embarrassment she felt spreading across her cheeks as she listened to his toast. His words thrilled her, caused her heart to pound just a little faster and her pulse to quicken. Maybe there was a chance after all, maybe he really did feel something special for her. But could he love her as much as she loved him? Was it even possible? Again the clouds of doubt and distrust tried to invade her thoughts, clouds carrying the impressions of her father's suicide and the disposition of his company. She didn't want to think about it, not at that time…perhaps not ever.

They relaxed in the hot tub. The heady sensations resulting from the hot swirling water combined with the champagne tugged at their nerve endings creating an increased sense of longing and hunger. Both felt the unmistakable pull, the sensual stirrings deep inside. They were enveloped in a cloud of steam, encased in a heated oneness of desire.

The empty champagne bottle settled into what remained of the ice at the bottom of the bucket. Paige and Bryce had allowed the tantalizing excitement to build between them. They kissed playfully and they kissed seriously, they touched everywhere as they intimately explored each other's body relishing the feel of slick, wet skin being gently massaged by the churning waters of the hot tub.

It was a time of quiet togetherness, quiet in the sense that few words were spoken. It was a quiet they both knew would soon erupt into the hot passion that simmered just below the surface, a passion that bordered on overwhelming. If ever there was a heated passion that could literally burst into flame, it existed between Paige and Bryce. It almost overpowered their ability to think. It filled the room until there was no room left.

He reached around her and gently gathered both breasts in his hands as she snuggled her body between his legs. She rested her hands along his thighs and leaned back against his chest. He nuzzled the side of her neck, then whispered in her ear, his voice thick with the urgency of his desire. "I think we've been in the water long enough."

She reached her hands up and placed them on top of his while running her foot along his calf. Her words were breathless. "I think so, too."

They stood up and stepped out of the hot tub. She shivered as the cool air hit her wet skin. He picked up a large towel and dried her off, then wrapped it around her, pausing long enough to place a soft kiss on her lips before quickly drying himself.

Bryce scooped Paige up in his arms and carried her to the loft, gently depositing her in the middle of the bed. There was no hesitancy in what they wanted, no tentative gestures or halting explorations. He buried his face between her breasts before hungrily taking her nipple into his mouth. He cupped her other breast in his hand, then slid his hand down her rib cage to her hip.

Just touching the silky smoothness of her skin excited him. He trailed the tip of his tongue from the underside of her breast down her stomach to the core of her femininity where he placed the most intimate of kisses.

She managed a quick intake of breath followed by a moan of pure pleasure. Her blood raced hot through her veins. Bryce brought out passions in her she had never before known existed, passions beyond what she thought were possible. She reveled in his attentions, every place he touched her creating sensual waves of ecstasy.

He rolled onto his back, taking her with him so that she straddled his body with her knees on either side of his thighs. She saw the heated desire burning in the depths of his eyes, a longing that beckoned to her. She leaned forward, slowly running her hands across his shoulders. Her ragged breathing matched the labored rise and fall of his chest. She placed soft kisses across his shoulder and down his chest. His pounding heart reverberated against her mouth. She dipped her head lower and provocatively caressed his hardened arousal with her lips.

He jerked his head back into the pillow and squeezed his eyes shut. A deep growl of rapture clawed its way out of his throat. He wanted all of her. He wanted to possess her as much as he wanted to be possessed by her, both body and soul.

He grabbed her hips, lifted and slowly lowered her onto his rigidity. When her tightness encased him, a hard jolt of frenzied excitement shot through him. The words slipped out in a husky whisper. "Paige...I..." He managed to stop the rest before saying more than he wanted to. He guided her with his hands and his hips until they moved together as one in a sensual mating barely holding to the constraints of reality.

She closed her eyes and allowed him to guide her into a rhythm and movement designed to set her very nerve endings on fire with a type of electrifying sensation totally new to her. She threw back her head and gasped for air as the convulsions claimed her. Once again he had transported her to the farthest reaches of euphoria, filling her with the depth and intensity of his ardor.

The rise and fall of his hips became more insistent, his control losing out to his all-consuming physical needs. He wrapped his arms around her, drawing her body down on top of his. He turned over so that he was on top of her, carefully preserving the connection of his hardness embedded deep inside her. His thrusts became quicker, his ragged breathing turned labored. With one final deep thrust the hard spasms raced through his body leaving him gasping for air.

He held her tightly, not wanting to break the tangible thread still binding them physically together. He fought to bring his breathing under control and was finally able to claim her mouth with a kiss that spoke as much of love as it did passion.

Their sensibilities slowly returned to normal as they cuddled together in the afterglow of their joined bodies. It was all so natural, so comfortable and felt so very right. It was a time of quiet reflection, soft kisses, intimate touching and murmured exchanges continuing long into the night until sleep finally claimed them.

Eight

Paige and Bryce had already taken an early-morning run down the mountain and were on their way back up in the ski lift for a second run. The clear morning sky sparkled with blue brilliance, the snow glistened in the bright sun, the crisp air smelled of pine trees. The spring snow conditions were perfect and the midweek crowds were at a minimum, which made the lift lines short. It had been an exhilarating run they had both enjoyed.

There was just enough time for one more run down the slope before lunch. They stood poised at the top of the hill. They had decided on one of the side runs. It was a little more difficult than what Paige was accustomed to but, since no one else was on it, Bryce promised to take it easy and help her.

They pushed off. The pristine powder conditions made things easy and comfortable. It was a long run. Bryce was a little ahead of Paige so he stopped to wait for her to catch

up. He watched as she came into view. Then he heard it—
the unmistakable roar as tons of snow broke loose from
high up the mountain. The noise filled the air. The wall of
snow gained momentum as it crashed down the mountain-
side, taking out everything in its path.

Paige heard it too and glanced back over her shoulder.
Her heart pounded in her throat. Her mouth went dry. She
saw it—a huge mass of snow high above and headed down
the slope. Her mind went blank for a brief moment, then
something finally clicked in her head bringing her back to
reality. All she could think of was *sideways,* she had to
move sideways to get clear of the path of the onrushing
snow. It was almost upon her. She turned, moving as fast
as she could. The deafening noise filled her head. The rush
of wind that preceded the wall of snow hit her hard. Everything went white as the snow crashed around her. Then
everything went black.

Bryce saw it all as it unfolded. He struggled to move
toward her, but it was impossible. The bitter taste of fear
filled his mouth. Not fear for his own safety, but fear for
Paige. He frantically clawed his way through the snow and
debris. He had been far enough to the side to be out of the
main path of the avalanche, but had still been tossed
around. There was a bleeding gash on his arm where something had ripped through his clothes and his ankle felt
tender as he tried to stand on it. None of that mattered.
Nothing mattered to him except finding Paige.

He had seen her move as she tried to get out of the path
of the crashing wall of snow. Then he lost sight of her. He
scrambled up the hill toward the spot where he had last
seen her. "Paige! Can you hear me? Paige! Paige!" He
kept calling to her, hoping against hope that she had been
thrown clear, that she could hear him, that she could answer him.

He finally made his way to the spot where he had last seen her. He searched the area, tugging at tree branches and digging through piles of snow with his hands as he searched for any sign. He refused to acknowledge the throbbing in his ankle or his bleeding arm. He finally forced a calming breath as he desperately tried to put some logic to the problem and to stop his frantic, scattered activities.

He looked around. She had been on the very edge, the main path of the destruction would have passed by her. He had seen her move even farther away. He again looked around, trying to get his bearings. Landmarks—trees, bushes, rocks—much of it had been ripped out and carried away or left covered by snow. He tried to focus his thinking. There had to be something, some way to—

The breath stilled in his lungs and his heart stopped for a moment. Off to the side, a hint of something bright red caught his eye. Paige had been wearing a red ski cap, red jacket and red pants. His heart started to pound like a jackhammer. He could taste the adrenaline. He rushed to the spot, half stumbling, half crawling. He reached for the bit of red. His hand closed around the knit fabric and pulled it out of the snow.

Paige's ski cap yanked free. He stared at it for a moment, then shoved it in his pocket. She had to be somewhere close. With the location of the ski cap as the center, he combed the surrounding area in an ever-increasing arc extending down the hill and out to the side following the direction of the avalanche. Doubts and fears plagued him. What if he had not searched thoroughly enough and passed her by? Or, what if he took too long searching in one place and would not find her in time? He angrily shoved the thoughts aside. There was no *if*. He *would* find her.

His heart skipped a beat, then almost stopped when he saw the bright red color where he had just scooped some

snow away. Frantically, like a man possessed, Bryce
clawed at the snow. A leg, another leg, then her entire body.
He pulled her free. A cold shiver of panic swept through
him. He held her tightly against his body. She was so pale,
so cold—so lifeless. The snow matted in her hair showed
the dark red of blood. He quickly brushed the snow from
her face, then tried to find a pulse. Nothing—no, wait a
minute. There it was. Very faint, but a pulse.

She felt so cold. He had to get her somewhere warm and
quick. If her body temperature continued to drop she could
die from hypothermia. He tried to determine where the
blood was coming from. If the wound was bad enough,
then she could bleed to death. Perhaps her subnormal body
temperature had slowed the bleeding. It was like being
caught between the proverbial rock and hard place. If he
did not get her body temperature up she could die from the
cold, yet it might have been the cold that kept her from
bleeding to death.

He did not have time to speculate. He knew he could not
carry her through the snow, it would be too slow and cum-
bersome. Both pairs of skis had been lost. He quickly gathered as many small branches as he could find and wove
them together. He could make better time by pulling the
makeshift sled behind him. He shook the snow from her
ski cap and put it back on her. At least he could slow down
the major loss of body heat through the top of her head.

Bryce thought a moment, then recalled the emergency
ski patrol hut he had seen earlier that morning. He knew it
was close by. Scanning the surrounding area he quickly got
his bearings, then settled on a direction and route. He
trudged through the snow carefully pulling his precious
cargo behind him, refusing to give in to the painful throbbing of his arm and ankle.

It seemed like forever, when Bryce finally spotted the

hut. Very soon now he would have a fire going and would have her wrapped in warmth. Then it would be a matter of waiting for help.

He finally reached the hut and shoved the door open. He breathed a sigh of relief when he found it stocked with emergency provisions. Firewood had been piled up next to the fireplace, lanterns were intact, blankets and sleeping bags were folded in the corner and there were canned goods on a shelf. Then his gaze lit on the one thing he needed most at that moment—a first-aid kit.

Bryce picked Paige up from the makeshift sled and carried her inside. She hung limp in his arms, still unconscious and lifeless. He quickly wrapped some blankets around her and laid her on the cot, then went immediately to the fireplace. As soon as he had a roaring blaze going, he grabbed the first-aid kit. He needed to get some kind of bandage wrapped around her head to help stop the bleeding when her body started warming up. As soon as he had accomplished that, he took stock of what else he could do.

The fire, in addition to warming the hut, would act as a signal. Someone would spot the smoke coming from the chimney. The one important thing that needed to be done now was to get Paige's body temperature up. It did not matter how many blankets he wrapped around her, they would not help much. All they could do was prevent her own body heat from escaping which is what normally would have kept her warm. The problem was that her body was not generating enough heat. The only thing to do was share his body heat with her, let the heat he generated radiate to her.

He quickly removed her clothes and his own clothes, then zipped their bodies together inside a sleeping bag. He shivered as her cold skin came in contact with his. He wrapped his arms around her and held her close to his heat, rubbing his hands across the surface of her skin to stimulate circulation.

He did not like it that she had not regained consciousness. A new fear settled deep inside him. What if she slipped into a coma? He had to get through to her, had to somehow stimulate her mind.

"Paige, can you hear me? Listen to my voice. Concentrate. You can do it. I'll tell you what. When we get out of here let's go someplace nice and warm. Maybe Hawaii…or Tahiti."

He pulled her tighter against his body, gently held her head against his shoulder, then closed his eyes. He continued to talk to her, not knowing whether or not she could hear him. "We'll bask in the warming rays of the sun on the white sand beaches of some deserted island. We'll allow the balmy tropical breezes to caress our skin, the palm trees will fan away our every care. The night sky will cover us, a million stars will twinkle in the heavens, each point of brilliance directed to your pleasure. We'll walk on the beach in the early-morning light and make love to the sound of the waves gently lapping against the sand. I promise I won't take any work with me. Not even a cell phone. It will be just the two of us."

He continued to talk to her. He talked about everything that came into his mind, he talked nonstop. He told her about the puppy he had when he was a little boy. He told her about his parents who were retired and lived in Florida. He told her about his inner desires. He talked about his fears, things he had never shared with another living soul. He told her of his fear that it was too late for him to have a family of his own, how he never thought he would ever find the right woman to share his life. "—and now that I've found that person…don't leave me, Paige. I couldn't bear to lose you, I don't know how I'd be able to go on."

He continued to talk, half of what he said did not really make any sense, but he knew he had to continue to talk, to say words to her, to stimulate her mind so that it would not close down. He had never felt so helpless in his life.

Then he heard voices and a minute later the door of the hut swung open and members of the Search and Rescue team poured in. Bryce squeezed his eyes tightly shut as the overwhelming elation enveloped him. He made a mental note to make a large donation to the Search and Rescue program, whatever it was that they needed. Perhaps enough for a helicopter. The rescue party quickly took charge of the situation, transporting Bryce and Paige to the hospital.

The hospital was a bustling hive of activity, most of it centering around the emergency room. Bryce's attitude was insistent, his tone of voice demanding as he talked to the admitting clerk. "Look, I'm not about to sit around in this waiting room. I intend to stay in there with Paige until I know she's going to be okay."

The clerk's manner was brisk, she had better things to do than argue with this unreasonable man. "Those are the rules, Mr. Lexington. What I suggest you do with your time while you're waiting is to let us take care of your injuries." She indicated the laceration on his arm and the way he was favoring his ankle.

"If you have people standing around with nothing better to do than take care of minor little cuts and sprains, then they should be tending to Paige rather than concerning themselves with me." His words were emphatic.

The clerk's demeanor softened when the extent of his anxiety and concern became obvious. "Everything that can be done is being done. Neglecting your own injuries won't help her. Now, why don't you let Dr. Harrington take a look at your arm and ankle?"

Bryce reluctantly allowed the doctor to take care of the

gash on his arm and check his ankle. The laceration required ten stitches, his ankle was badly sprained, but nothing was torn or broken. The doctor wrapped it. Following his treatment, Bryce paced up and down the hallway outside the emergency room. He refused to sit down and stay off his ankle even though it throbbed painfully.

After what seemed like eternity, Paige was taken to a room. It had been several hours since she was first transported to the hospital. Her vital signs were stable and she seemed to be resting comfortably, but she still had not regained consciousness. Bryce sat in the chair next to her bed, holding her hand. He looked at the machines monitoring her condition, the IV hooked up to her arm. He pictured her laughing face, thought of the previous night when they had made love so passionately. It all seemed like such a long time ago, so much had happened in the last twelve hours. He continued to talk to her until he fell asleep in the chair by her bed.

The duty nurse conferred with the doctor in the hallway outside Paige's room. "He's sleeping in the chair next to her bed. I wanted to make him more comfortable, but he refuses to leave her side."

The doctor leaned against the wall and stifled a yawn. It had been a long day and he was tired. "According to the information I received from Search and Rescue, he definitely saved her life. He did absolutely everything that could be done and did it right. It's truly a miracle that he was able to find her at all and that she's alive. Now it's a matter of time. We'll have to wait and see if she regains consciousness."

"Bryce…are you awake?"

He shook the grogginess from his head and opened his eyes, squinting at the early-morning sun flooding through the window into the hospital room. He focused on Joe Thompkins. "Yeah, I'm awake."

Bryce's voice conveyed his weariness. His face was drawn and haggard. A three-day growth of beard stubbled his face. He had not left Paige's room, not even once, during that three-day period of time. He reached for her hand, clasping it between his two hands. Three days and she still had not regained consciousness. After forty-eight hours it was officially considered a coma. He lifted her hand to his lips, tenderly kissing her palm.

"I'm sorry, Bryce. Is there anything I can do?"

Bryce held Paige's hand against his chest and closed his eyes for a moment, then looked at Joe. "No. Everything that can be done has been. Now it's just a matter of waiting."

Joe placed his hand on Bryce's shoulder and gave it a squeeze. "Try to get some rest."

"Yeah...sure." He turned his attention back to Paige, rising from the chair and standing next to her bed. He reached out and smoothed her hair back, being careful not to touch the small gash on the side of her head. It had not been as serious as Bryce had thought, not even requiring any stitches. The blood he had seen was all there was, the wound had not started bleeding again.

"Paige...can you hear me? Answer me...please answer me...say something." He continued to talk to her, continued to hold her hand, continued to caress her face. It had been three days, each day his despair increased. Bryce Lexington—the dynamic man in charge of all that went on around him—could not do anything to change the circumstances. No amount of power, authority or money could make any difference. All he could do was wait.

Morning passed into afternoon and afternoon into early evening. Bryce was where he had been the entire time, at

Paige's side. Joe Thompkins entered the room, pausing at the door to compose himself. He had traveled to Aspen as soon as Bryce had called him. The look of despair on Bryce's face tugged at his insides. Joe had been with Bryce for a long time. The ex-policeman had a great deal of respect for his employer, he knew him to be a fair and honest man. Many of the unheralded acts of generosity Bryce did for people were handled through Joe rather than normal office channels. They were the things Bryce wanted done quietly so as not to embarrass the recipients of his charity, not the least of whom had been Joe himself.

The young police officer had been the one who'd responded to a burglary call at Bryce's office. The two men struck up an immediate friendship. A couple of years later Joe's wife had died and he had been at an absolute loss, sinking into a deep depression. He had taken medical leave from the police force, but had been unable to pull himself together. When it became apparent to Bryce that Joe was not trying to combat his depression, was making no attempt to get back into the mainstream of society and get on with his life, he went to Joe's apartment and physically removed him against his will.

For the next six months Joe had lived at Bryce's house. Each day a psychologist had come to the house to conduct therapy sessions. Bryce had pushed Joe into becoming involved in various activities his company sponsored—the softball team, the bowling league, community service projects. Slowly but surely Joe had regained his former enthusiasm for life and his desire to be part of the world. There was nothing he would not do for the man who had literally pulled him up from the depths of self-destruction.

Now it was Joe's turn to repay the debt. "You can't stay here like this, Bryce. Go back to the house and get some sleep. I'll stay here. If there's any change I'll call you immediately. You're not doing yourself any good by living in this chair. Paige is going to be all right.''

Joe took hold of Bryce's arm and gave it a tug. ''Come on, let me drive you back to the house.''

Bryce jerked his arm out of Joe's grasp. ''No!'' His voice grew louder. ''I'm not leaving here until she regains consciousness!''

''What's all the noise?'' The voice was weak, the words barely audible.

Almost uncontrollable tremors darted through Bryce's body as he whirled toward the bed. His own voice was no louder than a whisper as he bent over the bed and took her hand in his. ''Paige?'' He saw the confusion in her eyes as she looked around the room, then settled her gaze on him again.

''Bryce? What's going on? Where am I?'' She reached up and touched his whiskered cheek, then let her hand drop to her side. She offered a weak smile. ''What have you been doing? Pardon my saying so, but you look a mess.''

He immediately pressed the call button for the nurse. The joy, the total and complete elation he felt at that moment, welled inside him until he thought he would burst. He sat on the edge of her bed, his hands trembled as he cupped her face. He had not cried since he was ten years old, but he could not stop the tears of joy that filled his eyes and threatened to spill over and trickle down his cheeks. His voice teased. ''Oh, yeah? Well, you're no beauty queen at the moment either.''

Joe's voice was quiet, but the happiness he felt could not be hidden. ''Well...you don't need me here.'' He turned to leave just as the nurse entered the room. He gestured toward the bed. ''It's good news.''

The nurse immediately called for the doctor, then turned to Bryce. ''If you'll excuse us, Mr. Lexington.''

"Sure." He leaned forward and kissed Paige on the cheek, then squeezed her hand. "I'll see you in a bit." For the first time since she was placed in the room, he left and went out into the hallway.

"Well, now…how are we feeling?" The nurse adjusted the drip on the IV and straightened the blanket on Paige's bed. "You're a very lucky young lady." She glanced around to make sure Bryce had left the room. "He hasn't left your bedside for three days."

"Three days? I've been here for three days?" The surprise and confusion twisted Paige's face into a frown. She tried to think, to force some memory of how and why she came to wake up in a hospital. "What happened? The last thing I remember was being on the ski lift going up the mountain."

"You were caught in an avalanche." The nurse paused as the doctor entered the room.

"Hello, Paige. It's very good to see you awake. We've been worried about you." The doctor quickly read the chart hanging on the end of her bed. "Let's check a few things."

While the doctor and nurse busied themselves, the nurse continued to fill Paige in on the series of events from her last memory to the present. Forty-five minutes passed before the doctor gave her a smile and a pat on the arm and told her she was going to be just fine. He assured her that she could be released from the hospital in another day or so.

After the doctor and nurse left her room, Paige mulled over everything the nurse had told her about what Bryce had done. The nurse had been very specific, saying that Paige literally owed her life to Bryce's decisive actions. She also told her of Bryce's devotion, how he had not left her side from the moment she was placed in the room, how he had initially refused treatment for his own injuries until he was sure she was being properly tended to.

Tears filled her eyes. Bryce had stayed by her side for three days. She knew how many business projects he was involved with, how many things required his attention, but he had abandoned all of it and stayed with her. She closed her eyes. A million thoughts and feelings whirled through her.

She tried to sort it all out, what was real and what was probably some sort of dream. She distinctly remembered hearing his voice coming to her from out of the darkness. So many things swirled around in her head. There was a vivid mental picture of a lush tropical beach, the warm ocean breezes. She had fuzzy thoughts about a little boy and a puppy, something about being in Florida. All the thoughts centered around Bryce. She remembered hearing his words of devotion and caring, at least she thought she remembered. Maybe she just wanted it so much that she imagined it to be true.

There were other thoughts, ones not so pleasant. Dark thoughts about her father and his suicide, thoughts about how Bryce fit into everything, what type and how much responsibility he had in her father's downfall. They were confused thoughts. She didn't want to believe that Bryce had any involvement, but she couldn't shake the thought.

"Paige? Are you awake?" Bryce's voice was soft. He wanted desperately to talk to her, to know for himself that she was all right, but he did not want to disturb her.

She opened her eyes and focused on him. His face was drawn and haggard, but the relief he was experiencing could not be hidden. His eyes were tired, but they sparkled with happiness. She reached her hand out toward him. "Yes, I'm awake."

He took her hand in his and sat on the edge of the bed.

He lovingly smoothed her hair away from her face and caressed her cheek. "How are you feeling?" Once again he felt the emotion well inside him. As much as he wanted to share his inner feelings, to tell her of his love, he still could not force out the proper words.

"From what I'm told, if it weren't for you I wouldn't be feeling anything ever again." The overwhelming emotion filled her reality as it fought to get out. Her voice quavered as she spoke. "You saved my life. How does someone repay something like that?"

He looked into the honesty of her eyes. He wanted to take her into his arms, but she was still hooked up to too many tubes and wires. He had to be content with just holding her hand. He tried to cover his own deeply emotional state by teasing her. "There's nothing to repay, it was self-defense. You've made such a mess of my computer files that I have to keep you around until you straighten them out so I can find things again."

She smiled at him, returning his teasing. "That's not inefficiency on my part, that's job security."

"Well, whatever it is…" He could not keep up the teasing any longer, his emotions were too strong. She would be all right, he could take her home in a day or so. Home…that was what he wanted, a home and a family with Paige. That was what would finally make his life complete.

He quickly regained his composure. She had already been through a lot, now was not the time to put an additional burden on her. Now was not the time to tell her of his love or to ask her to make a decision concerning any type of commitment. He would wait until she had fully recovered, wait until they were home.

The butterflies in his stomach only confirmed what he already knew. He was scared. He wanted this very much, more than he had ever wanted anything before in his life.

It was also something over which he had no control. If anything went wrong, if things did not go the way he wanted...he was scared.

The next two days passed without incident. Bryce was finally willing to leave the hospital to go back to the rented house and get some much-needed sleep. With Paige's regained strength and the fact that she was able to eat solid food without any problem, the doctor said she was well enough to leave. He discharged her from the hospital and an orderly pushed her in a wheelchair out to the curb where Bryce had the car waiting. He had packed their personal belongings, everything was in the truck. They drove to the airport and were on their way home shortly after settling into Bryce's private jet.

"How are you feeling?" He fussed around her like a mother hen tending to her chicks. "Is there anything you need?" He tucked a blanket around her.

"What I need—" she could not stop the smile from turning the corners of her mouth "—is for you to stop treating me like an invalid. I feel fine."

"Are you sure? You know what the doctor said, you have to take it easy for a few days."

"How am I supposed to relax when you keep fussing over me?"

"Humor me for a while. Now, when we get back I'm going to have a nurse—"

"A nurse!" The shocked expression on her face said it all. "Bryce Lexington, don't you dare get a nurse for me! I'm perfectly all right, I can walk and talk and function just fine. If you don't stop this..." She searched for some sort of strong statement that would let him know emphatically how she felt about it. "Well...if you don't stop bullying me I'll just have to get out of this plane and walk home."

He could not stop the laughter as he glanced out the window. "From thousands of feet up in the air?"

"Yes!" She tried to glare at him, but couldn't hide her amusement at how silly that really sounded.

He sat next to her on the couch, taking her hand in his. He continued to chuckle softly. "You really think I'm being that ridiculous?"

"I don't think, I *know*."

He took a deep breath as his concern returned. "All right, I'll offer you a compromise, but this is the only concession I'm going to make so you'd better accept it or we go back to my original plan of getting a nurse for you." He ran his fingertips lightly across her cheek before cupping her chin in his hand. "I want you to stay at my house for a few days where I can keep an eye on you. It will give you a chance to build up your strength and gain back the weight you lost. You may say you feel fine, but you're not one hundred percent yet." He gazed into the depths of her eyes, then leaned forward to place a soft kiss on her lips.

"I want you close to me so that when you begin to have flashes of your lost memory from the time just prior to the accident, like the doctor said you would, I'll be there to help you through them, fill in the blanks." He leaned forward and brushed his lips softly against hers again. "Do we have a deal?"

The intensity of his eyes delved into her soul, touched her innermost thoughts and feelings. She really did not feel up to par, she knew her stamina was not what it should be and that she tired easily. Just the exertion of leaving the hospital and settling into the plane left her wanting to sit down and rest. She had spent five days in a hospital bed, three of those days unconscious. He was correct about her needing to build her strength.

She reached out and touched his cheek, then offered him a smile of resignation. "Okay, but only on one condition."

"What's that?"

"Each day will be a workday. There's lots to do, five lost days to catch up."

He eyed her carefully for a moment. "Half days only."

"No good. Regular workdays, I promise to stop if I get too tired."

"Okay, we'll try it your way." He brushed his lips against hers again, then smiled. "Remind me to send you next time I have labor negotiations to handle."

They went straight from the airport to Bryce's house. Without consulting her, he immediately put her things in his bedroom rather than a guest room. "Now—" he put his hands on her shoulders and pulled her close to him "—why don't you go out by the pool and soak up some of this nice warm sunshine while I check in with Eileen."

"Okay, warm sunshine sounds good. But, first thing to-morrow morning it's back to work for me."

Paige impulsively picked the skimpy red swimsuit. She started toward the pool, paused and looked toward the house, then went to Bryce's office. She checked the fax machine for messages, quickly glancing through those that had accumulated, until one jumped out in front of her. There, across the top of the page, in bold letters were the words Franklin Industries and a notation from Ben Jordan reminding Bryce of the board meeting in three days where the primary topic would be the company reorganization.

Paige's hand shook as she stared at the paper. She was so crazy in love with Bryce that she had almost succeeded in forcing her questions and concerns from her mind. But here they were again, confronting her and reminding her that there were still so many things left unanswered. She set the fax aside. For a brief moment she was sorry she had come across it. She changed into the swimsuit, went out to the pool and situated herself on a lounge chair. She closed her eyes, hoping the sun would warm the sadness that had suddenly chilled her insides.

Bryce observed her from a distance, then went over to the lounge chair and stood next to it as he continued to watch her. She seemed to be asleep, lying peacefully with her eyes closed. Even though she wore the red thong bikini that made his heart pound with desire, she seemed so delicate and fragile. When he thought of how close he had come to losing her, a cold chill darted up his spine. She was the one perfect woman for him, there could never be anyone else.

Paige was jarred out of her light sleep when his weight came down on the lounge chair next to her. She raised her hand to shade her eyes from the sun, then smiled at him. "You caught me, I must have dozed off."

"It's perfectly understandable, you've been through a lot lately. I brought some lunch, are you hungry?"

"I'm famished. I never realized how much I liked to eat until I was in the hospital. All those liquids just weren't the same as real sink-your-teeth-into-it food."

"Come on—" he held out his hand to help her up from the lounger "—I've set everything on the table."

They enjoyed a late lunch. The sun felt good on her skin, warm and relaxing. After they ate, Bryce disappeared into his office. She wanted to go with him, get busy on whatever work needed to be done, but he refused. He insisted that she relax in the warm sun. Paige reclaimed the lounge chair and settled into a comfortable position.

Her body might have been relaxed but her mind remained quite active. It kept going back to the fax about the reorganization of Franklin Industries. It was the first bit of new information she had come across. Everything she had been able to find in the computers had been standard accounting information, nothing helpful, nothing that told her what had happened between Bryce and her father or what Bryce intended to do with the company.

Had the confrontation she had managed to put out of her mind now come back to haunt her? Would she find herself torn between the man she loved and the reality of what had happened between him and her father? If Bryce did have something to do with what had happened to her father, how would she ever be able to live with that truth? The unpleasant and distasteful thoughts continued to circulate through her mind, giving rise to a new level of anxiety.

Nine

The sun dipped low in the sky and the air began to turn cool. Paige changed out of the swimsuit and put on a pair of jeans and a shirt. She went to Bryce's office and found him on the phone. When she stepped through the door he motioned her over to him.

He slipped his arm around her waist and pulled her down so that she was seated on his lap. As soon as he finished his phone conversation he wrapped his other arm around her so that she was fully in his embrace. His voice was soft, his manner loving. "Would you like to go to a movie tonight? There's several good films playing. Or, if you'd rather, we can rent a video."

"I'd just like to spend a quiet night at home." As soon as she said the words their full impact hit her. She felt the flush cover her cheeks, felt the embarrassment well inside her. "I mean...uh...if you don't mind, I'd rather not go out." Then she quickly added, "Of course, if you want to go somewhere please don't feel that you need to stay home because I'm here. I don't want my presence to cause you any inconvenience or make you feel you need to change your plans."

He liked the sound of what she had said, *spending a quiet night at home*. It sounded so settled, so comfortable, so much the way he wanted things to be with them. He closed his eyes and held her warmth tight against his body. He visualized what he hoped the future held, the two of them sharing their lives.

He finally found his voice. "Staying home sounds good to me, too." The quiet moment following and the implication of the words both of them had used permeated the air, instilling the emotion each was experiencing.

They spent the evening talking and listening to music. They shared personal remembrances from childhood, the hopes and dreams of their youth. When it came time to go to bed there was no awkwardness or embarrassment. They went upstairs together, each felt comfortable and content with the situation as if it was the most natural thing to be doing. He held her hand as they entered the bedroom.

They lay in bed next to each other, his arm around her shoulder and her head against his shoulder. His actions were tentative, unsure. He placed a soft kiss on her lips, caressed her cheek with his fingertips, then allowed his hand to slide down the side of her neck. As much as he wanted to make love to her, he was afraid to. He knew she needed to rest. He cradled her body next to his, kissed her tenderly on the cheek, closed his eyes and drifted off to sleep.

He did not know how long he had been sleeping when her erratic thrashing woke him. He sat bolt upright, fully awake and immediately aware of her mumbled words and the contorted mask of terror that covered her face even though she was still asleep. "Bryce…it's…help me." She frantically clawed at the covers in an attempt to escape whatever has happening in her mind at that moment.

He held her close to him, stroking her hair and talking softly. "It's okay, Paige. You're safe, I'm with you." He felt her body tremble as she put her arms around him.

Her voice sobbed as she spoke. "Pieces…pictures…just bits of things. I came around the turn, saw you down the hill waiting for me. The noise…the loud roar…all that snow."

"It's all right. The doctor said it would come back to you." He continued to stroke her hair and hold her body against his, easing her back into the softness of the bed so that she was lying down again. "He said it would take about seventy-two hours before you'd start remembering and that it would come back a little at a time." He brushed back a loose strand of hair. "Can I get you anything?"

Her voice was calmer, the initial panic was gone. "No, nothing. Just…" She looked up at him, her expression showing her tenuous emotional state. Her eyes questioned him before she spoke. "Could you just hold me for a little while?"

He flashed her a comforting smile. "Just try and stop me." He stretched out next to her, pulled the cover up around her shoulders and wrapped her in his warm embrace. "Now, just close your eyes and relax. You'll be asleep again before you know it." A warm, tingling sensation spread across his skin from the place where she rested her hand on his bare chest.

The rest of the night passed without incident. Paige slept peacefully until well after eight o'clock the next morning. When she woke and realized how late it was, she hurried to dress and get out to the office. She found Bryce hard at work.

"Why did you let me sleep so late? How long have you been working?"

He immediately rose from his chair and crossed the room to greet her. "You needed the rest." He put his arm around her shoulder and escorted her to the couch. As soon as she was seated, he poured her a cup of coffee and handed it to her.

She sipped the hot coffee, a thoughtful expression on her face. "It's all very strange. I know what happened, I was told. But, to go through something like that and not remember a thing about it and then suddenly have it pop into my head as such a vivid picture..."

"I know. This must be very difficult for you."

"I'm glad you insisted I stay here." She set down her coffee cup and looked into his caring face. "I'm so thankful that you were with me last night, it made things so much easier. I was very frightened for a few minutes, but you made everything all right."

He caressed her cheek, then traced the outline of her upper lip with the tip of his finger. The emotionally charged moment filled the air. Neither of them spoke for several minutes. They were content to bask in the warmth of the emotions surrounding them before turning to a busy workday.

Twice during the day she paused to rest for a little while. Bryce hovered around her, making sure she had everything she wanted. He tried to get her to go to the house and take a nap, but she refused saying all she needed was a few moments to sit and rest. He made no mention of the upcoming board meeting concerning her father's company and she did not ask about it. She was afraid of what answers he might give her.

That evening they watched a musical special on television. It was only nine o'clock when they turned off the lights downstairs and went up to the bedroom. They quickly undressed and were soon snuggled together in the warmth of the bed.

"Paige, I…" As much as he wanted to stroke the silkiness of her skin, tease her nipple to a deliciously taut peak, as much as he wanted to make love to her, he hesitated. "Are you—"

"Please…don't ask me if I'm feeling okay." She turned on her side and placed her hand against his chest. She felt the rise and fall of his breathing. "I don't need to be pampered, there's nothing wrong with me. I had an accident and was in the hospital for a couple of days, that's all."

He quickly corrected her attempt to lessen the significance and magnitude of what had happened. "Five days, not a couple of days—and three of them in a coma."

"All right, five days. But they released me and I'm feeling fine. Don't treat me like some fragile piece of crystal that will break at the slightest touch or a delicate flower that will wither and die if you so much as breathe on it. I'm a woman—"

His words were a breathless whisper. "Yes, you certainly are." His mouth captured hers with an unmistakable combination of passion and deep caring as his hand slid smoothly up her inner thigh.

His intimate touch ignited inside her. She melted into the excitement of his lovemaking. She stroked his strong shoulders and back, her foot rubbed against his bare calf as she tangled her leg with his. He was everything she wanted, everything she needed. With him her life would be perfect.

They would have a family, the children she'd never had with her ex-husband. Almost from the beginning it had been a bad marriage. In less than a year it became obvious to her that she had made a terrible mistake. Paige had decided that having children to save the marriage was both impractical and unfair to the innocent children who would be brought into the world. She wanted children, but she had decided to wait until she knew they would have a stable home.

Things went along in the rut of routine for another six years before she finally admitted that there was no marriage left to save. Her ex-husband pretended shock at the notion that there was something wrong with the marriage, a reaction that had angered her. All their conversations and discussions, her willingness to try a marriage counselor and his refusal to even consider it—there was no way he could have been surprised when she told him she wanted a divorce.

She had hoped the divorce would be civilized, but it was not to be. She had not asked for any support or any type of a settlement. She felt she was capable of taking care of herself and preferred to permanently sever all connections with that painful period of her life.

And now here was this perfect man, the answer to all her dreams. Did she want too much? Did she want more than she deserved? Did she want more than could be, more than what Bryce was willing to give? She didn't know what he wanted or how he felt. Was hers a love that would never be returned?

The warning of storm clouds still hovered on the horizon. There was the matter of Bryce Lexington's relationship with her father. She knew in the very depths of her heart and soul that Bryce was an honorable man. As much as she loved her father, she had started to suspect that the responsibility for what happened had to somehow fall on his shoulders, but she needed to know the truth.

All thoughts and concerns disappeared in a puff of smoke as he enclosed her tautly puckered nipple inside his mouth and gently suckled. She trailed her fingertips across the curve of his bottom.

Time and place had no meaning as they shared the infinite facets of their unspoken love. The warmth of that love filled the room. They moved in unison, their bodies in complete harmony, their souls merged into one.

Streaks of color invaded the early-morning sky. The weather forecast claimed another sunny, warm day. Bryce watched Paige as she slept in his arms. She had told him she needed to go back to her own apartment. The only clothes she had were what she had taken to Aspen and, even though they had been laundered, she needed to find a change of wardrobe. She also reminded him that her apartment had been closed up for over a week. She needed to check on things and make sure everything was okay. All her plants needed to be watered. He knew it was true, as far as it went, but he suspected there was more to her decision.

He had been awake half the night agonizing over this turn of events. His motives in bringing her back to his house were legitimate in the way he had presented them to her. He did want to make sure that she was fully recovered. But there was more. He thought if she was staying at his house that it would only be a short step to the arrangement becoming permanent. He berated himself for not having the courage to verbally express his emotions, to tell her how he felt rather than trying to manipulate her. As much as he wanted to tell her of his love, the risk of her not returning that love scared him equally.

Her decision to return to her own home so soon after they arrived back in Los Angeles had caught him by surprise. After giving it much thought, all he could think of was that he had rushed her into something she was not ready for. His concern that had first cropped up in London had been correct. The very real concern that had presented itself prior to the first time they had made love had been all too real. She must have felt pressured, felt as if she had no choice but to comply with his wishes.

He did not understand what the problem was, the real reason for her sudden decision to leave. He had tried to ask her, to get to the truth, but she'd insisted it was only to get herself together. He had never before in his life been so uncertain about what to do, how to proceed. If she was feeling pressured by him, then he did not want to compound the feeling by insisting on immediate answers. On the other hand, he could not just let her go. He watched her as she slept, trying to find any hint of what was going on inside her. When she began to stir, he tightened his embrace.

Paige slowly became aware of being awake and being in Bryce's arms. She felt so comfortable and protected. Her decision to go back to her apartment had not been an easy one. If she stayed, as he had suggested, then perhaps it would have been an easy transition to making it a permanent arrangement. It had been a very tempting offer, but one she knew she could not accept as long as there was still the unresolved matter of his involvement with her father and her concern for the jobs of the hundred employees of her father's company.

The upcoming board meeting concerning the reorganization of Franklin Industries might, at long last, provide her with some answers and put the matter to rest once and for all. She wanted to be able to confess to Bryce that she was Stanley Franklin's daughter, to erase the only secret she held from him other than the most important one of all—that she loved him with all her heart and soul.

Paige stirred, turned on her back and stretched her arms

and legs. She immediately felt his lips against her cheek as he gave her a kiss. She smiled and slowly opened her eyes. Her voice contained the thickness of sleep. "Good morning." She reached up and lightly touched her fingertips to his cheek.

"Good morning, yourself. Did you sleep well?"

"Perfectly." She closed her eyes again and allowed him to cradle her against his body. A brief thought flitted through her mind about wanting to spend the entire day right where she was, but she quickly dismissed it. "As delightful as this is, I've lots of work to do and should get started."

He gave her a teasing pat on her bare bottom, his eyes twinkled with amusement. "Won't that jerk you work for let you take the morning off? What is he, some kind of slave driver? Why do you work for a guy like that?"

"The job does have lots of fringe benefits—travel to exciting places, beautiful evening gowns, excellent medical benefits—" she glanced out the window toward the backyard "—and pool privileges." She returned his teasing smile. "Of course, the package also includes sleeping with the boss." She had said it as a joke, hoping to make him laugh. She saw the teasing sparkle quickly disappear from his eyes to be replaced with apprehension, anxiety and just a hint of pain.

He grasped her hand and pulled her down on the bed, but did not enfold her in his arms. She had forced some of his fears out into the open. "Paige..." He shook his head from side to side as a frown wrinkled his forehead. "Is that why you want to return to your own apartment? Do you feel that you're being coerced—"

"Absolutely not!" It had never occurred to her that he would take her teasing remark in that light. She slipped her arms around his neck and snuggled her body next to his.

"I only meant it in jest. In no way have you pressured me or made me feel uncomfortable."

The worry still lingered in his eyes. "Are you sure?"

"Yes, I'm positive."

He hoped what she said was what she really felt and believed. He did not see even a hint of concern or discomfort in her eyes or on her face. He hugged her to him, burying his face in her soft hair. "Okay." He gave her a tender kiss on the cheek, then released her from his embrace. He offered what he hoped was a confident smile. "Let's have some breakfast, then get to work."

He did not like the feelings he had been experiencing of late, feelings so foreign that they took a while for him to even identify. He finally figured out that what had been plaguing him was insecurity, something he had never before come across and was not sure exactly how to handle. He did not want to do anything wrong, did not want to rush her, did not want to take a chance on doing something that would cause her to turn away. If only he could find the courage to tell her of his love, to share that most precious and protected place he kept locked inside him.

He kept his fears and concerns carefully hidden as they embarked on a busy workday. They picked up the pieces of the Chicago project they had been involved with prior to leaving for Aspen. There were also follow-up details on the London art gallery project and the two artists in Aspen whose work would be going there.

Paige immediately got back into the swing of things. It was the first day since leaving the hospital that she felt one hundred percent. She enjoyed being productive and busy. Several times during the day Bryce had asked her if she was tired or if she would like to rest. His concern was touching, but it finally became too much. She had to tell him that if he asked her one more time she was going to scream.

She looked at her watch, then turned her attention to him. "I've put everything away and the computer is signed off for the night. So, if you wouldn't mind, I could use a ride home." She saw his eyes cloud, then the look quickly disappeared as he rose from his chair.

He took her hand, enclosing it between his two hands. "Are you sure you need to go back to your apartment?"

She placed her other hand on top of his. "Yes, you know I do. I haven't been there in over a week, I need—"

He tried to hide his disappointment. "I know, you need to water your plants."

Bryce reluctantly drove her home. After placing her suitcase in her bedroom he wrapped his arms around her. "I could wait while you water your plants, then we—"

She placed her fingertips against his lips. "I'll see you in the morning at seven o'clock."

He smiled at her. "You're a stubborn woman, Bradford." He placed a loving kiss on her lips. "I'll see you in the morning. Make it six-thirty, if that's not too early for you. I've got a board meeting at two o'clock and we've got lots to do before then."

"That's not too early. I'll see you then." She walked with him to her front door. They paused as he pulled her into his embrace and covered her mouth with his in a gentle kiss of loving care. He caressed her cheek with his fingertips, allowing a sigh of resignation before going through the door.

Paige closed the door and returned to her bedroom to unpack her suitcase. After putting everything away she went to the kitchen and popped a frozen dinner into the microwave. Bryce had wanted her to stay at his house for dinner. When she refused he tried to get her to stop somewhere and have dinner with him on her way home. Again she had declined his offer. She knew if she didn't go straight home that her resolve would weaken and she would end up spending the night at his house again. As much as she wanted to do just that, she knew she couldn't stay there another night.

Everything had happened so fast, enchanting things she had feared would never be a part of her life. Her dreams for the future suddenly loomed large in front of her rather than maintaining a position in some remote corner of her existence. Suddenly her hopes and desires seemed more than possible, they seemed very real. She closed her eyes and hugged her arms around her shoulders as a tremor darted through her body. Was she wanting more than she could have? More than she deserved? She busied herself taking care of chores. She watered her plants, then did her laundry, all the while wondering where her relationship with Bryce was headed, what kind of a relationship it really was and exactly what Bryce wanted. What if he didn't want any more than what they had right now? Could she live with that? It was a question that didn't have an immediate answer.

Upon leaving Paige's apartment, Bryce went directly home. He wanted to spend some quiet time organizing his thoughts about the restructuring of Franklin Industries before his meeting the next day. Despite pressure from his board of directors to liquidate the company, he wanted to save it. He felt confident that if he could come up with a plan that would have the company turning a profit in three years rather than five years, then the board would go along with it. He went out to his office, turned on the computer and began projecting figures for various cost-saving measures and looking at possible areas of market expansion. It was almost two in the morning when he turned off the computer and went to bed. He was pleased with what he had accomplished.

Paige arrived promptly at six-thirty the next morning, ready to work. The aroma of freshly brewed coffee greeted her as she entered the office. "That smells good, I could use a cup. I didn't have time to make any coffee before I left home. These early hours of yours don't allow for a leisurely breakfast."

As she poured herself a cup of coffee, Bryce came up behind her, pulled her hair aside and brushed his lips across the back of her neck, then wrapped his arms around her waist. His words were soft. "If you had stayed here last night you would have saved yourself the travel time this morning."

"It's a good thing I did go home. I don't know what was dustier, my plants or my furniture. Now my plants are happy and the dust has been removed from the furniture."

His words had touched a place deep inside her. She tried to cover her feelings with chitchat. She had felt so lost and alone as she had lain in bed trying to force herself to sleep. More than anything she had wanted to be wrapped in the warm security of his embrace as she slept.

A whole new feeling of confusion and uncertainty had enveloped her after he had left her apartment. Things had to be brought out in the open, had to be made clear. She could not go on suspended between two worlds, loving Bryce with all her heart and soul yet at the same time feeling so unsettled about the reason for her father's suicide and the future of his employees.

There was also that guilt inside her. She had taken the major step of giving Bryce her trust, but she had not given him her honesty. She had never told him she was Stanley

Franklin's daughter. He had accepted her on face value, trusting that she was exactly who she seemed to be. She had wondered if she could trust him, but the truth turned out to be just the opposite. She was the one who couldn't be trusted. The lies and deception tugged at her. The uncomfortable emotion shivered through her body.

"You're trembling." He turned her around so that she faced him. "Are you cold?"

She tried to cover her inner turmoil. "I guess a little. I dressed for the warm day that we're going to have, but it's still too early, it hasn't warmed up yet."

She moved quickly to start on the workday. He would be leaving at one-thirty for his board meeting. They were each involved with different projects. Paige worked on the Chicago proposal while Bryce prepared for the board meeting. He had disappeared into the private office at the back of the pool house office structure, leaving her in the front room. It was almost one-thirty when a fax came through marked Urgent. She retrieved the fax and took it to him.

"Sorry to break into your busy day..." Her voice trailed off as she grinned at the startled look on his face, a startled look that quickly turned sheepish. She had assumed he was working, taking care of important business. Instead, she found him playing a video game on the computer.

"You caught me." He glanced back at the monitor, then returned his attention to her. "I was about to break my old record."

"I thought you were in here working," her voice teased as she crossed the room and handed him the fax.

He took the paper from her, then grasped her hand and pulled her down onto his lap. His lips tickled across her cheek, then nibbled at the tender spot behind her ear. "You know what they say, *All work and no play*... Well, I felt in need of a little break from work so I took a crack at my old record.''

She glanced at the score flashing on the screen. It was, indeed, a very impressive achievement, as video games went. ''Is there anything you don't do well?''

His expression turned serious. He caressed her cheek and searched the depths of her eyes. He took a calming breath as he thought about her question. The answer was yes... there was definitely something he didn't do well. He didn't know how to express his emotions, how to talk about his personal inner feelings, how to get over his fear of allowing his vulnerability to show.

''Paige...'' He stroked her hair as he searched her face, then settled, again, on her eyes. ''I...'' This was a definite first for him. He was thirty-eight years old and had never before told a woman he loved her. He could not force her to love him, he could not negotiate it like a business deal. He had no way of exercising any power or authority over her emotions and feelings. He could only hope he was doing the right thing.

''Paige...I want to...we...'' His words choked off in his throat. His emotions overcame him and he was unable to continue with what he wanted to say. He glanced at the clock. It was late. He needed to leave. ''I've got to be going to my board meeting. Please wait here until I get back. We have things to talk about, important things that...well...'' He glanced awkwardly at the floor, then regained eye contact with her. ''Will you please wait?''

Was he talking about their relationship? Could he possibly be wanting to discuss their future together? Was she reading too much into what he had said? The almost overpowering emotions made it difficult for her to speak. Her words came out in a breathless whisper. ''Yes, I'll wait.''

''I should be back no later than four o'clock.''

Paige busied herself while Bryce was gone, taking care of updating the computer files. The afternoon moved at a snail's pace as anxiety churned inside her. Exactly what did Bryce want to discuss with her? What was so important that it couldn't wait until the next day? Her emotions vacillated between the exhilaration of believing he wanted them to have a future together and the despair of her fearing he wanted to tell her they had no future. She finally put everything away for the day and glanced at the clock.

It was ten minutes after four and Bryce had not yet returned to the house. The tension knotted in the pit of her stomach. She had not been honest with him. She needed to confess, to rid herself of the ever-growing guilt that ate away at her. He had been so open with her, so honest and so trusting. She owed him the same consideration. She could not have a relationship with him while this deception stood between them.

She knew what she had to do. As soon as he returned, before he had a chance to say anything, she would tell him who she was and what had first brought her to his place of business. She loved him so much, she had to clear up anything that might interfere with what she hoped would be their future together and she had to do it now before it was too late. An uneasy shiver darted through her body telling her more than she wanted it to. Was it already too late?

Bryce always had things entered into the computer immediately. She went into the computer files that contained the minutes of the board meetings. Perhaps that would tell her whether or not the meeting had been adjourned. She quickly found what she wanted. The report indicated that the board meeting had been over since three o'clock, almost an hour and a half ago. He should have been home an hour ago. She casually paged through the minutes, scanning but not really reading.

The words leaped off the screen, grabbing her total attention. The board had voted unanimously to rid the corporation of Franklin Industries. They had decreed it too costly to operate the company at a loss for the next five years. That could only mean one thing. The company would be liquidated and the employees would be fired.

Then the full impact penetrated her consciousness. It had been *unanimous*. Bryce had voted in favor of the motion, too. She felt a cold pain of betrayal stab through her. How could he so callously put one hundred people out of work for the sake of saving a few dollars? Those were not the actions of the man she had fallen in love with, not the actions of the man she had come to believe in. And even more important, the man she had placed her trust in.

Just when she had learned to trust again, it had all turned on her. The confusion ran rampant. She trembled violently and a sick sensation rose in her throat. She suddenly felt so terribly alone. Why hadn't he come home? What would she say to him when he finally arrived? She fought the urge to run and hide from the horrible pain churning inside her. The tears welled in her eyes. Where was he?

An impatient Bryce sat in the middle of the freeway in bumper-to-bumper traffic. He wanted to get back to Paige. They had many things to talk about and, he hoped, many plans to make for the future—their future together as husband and wife. It was going on four-thirty when he finally pulled into the garage. He was relieved to see Paige's car still parked in the driveway.

His relief was quickly replaced with panic when he stepped into the office. A look of complete despair covered her face as she stared at the computer screen. He rushed to her side, kneeling next to her chair. ''Paige...what's wrong?''

The sound of his voice and his sudden appearance startled her. She whirled to face him. Tears filled her eyes, her voice quavered. "Why? How could you…"

The pain and bewilderment he saw in her eyes was almost more than he could bear. A sinking feeling filled him with dread. He didn't know what was wrong, could not imagine what had happened during the few hours he had been gone. He put his hands on her shoulders and moved to embrace her. He swallowed down the lump in his throat as he tried to speak. "I don't understand what you're talking about. How could I do what?"

The tears finally overflowed and trickled down her cheeks as she shook loose from his grasp. She jumped to her feet and ran toward the door. She was so confused and heartsick, her entire world had crashed around her. She paused before leaving the office, paused long enough to turn toward him. "How could you do it? How could you put one hundred hardworking people out on the street?"

She waved her hand toward the computer screen as a sob caught in her throat. She blurted out the words, barely cognizant of what she was saying. "How can I trust someone who was somehow responsible for my father's suicide?" She turned and ran across the patio toward the house and the circular driveway in front. All she wanted at that moment was to get away from Bryce and from the pain.

Bryce stared after her in stunned silence before regaining his wits. It had all happened so fast. He glanced at the screen to see what she had been looking at and immediately recognized the minutes of the board meeting, the minutes going only as far as what had actually happened in the meeting, but making no mention of the separate meeting that had followed.

It hit him like a bolt of lightning. She didn't know about her father or what had happened. He sprang into action. He had to stop her before she could leave. There was so much to talk about, things that needed explaining.

He now had the missing piece. She had been seeking answers and had held him accountable for consequences that were the result of things beyond his control, things her father had done long before Bryce had become involved. He had not intended to share the facts he had uncovered concerning what Stanley Franklin had done, no purpose would be served by making the circumstances public knowledge. However, now things had changed. Nothing was more important to him than Paige. As much as he wanted to protect her from anything painful, if he had to reveal the truth to her in order to keep her, then that's what needed to happen.

As he reached the side door of the house he heard a car engine start. He frantically yanked open the door, dashed toward the alarm panel and slammed his hand against the switch that closed the electronic gates at the end of the long curving driveway. Her car was already halfway down the driveway when he emerged from the house.

Bryce raced across the front lawn toward the closing gates. An adrenaline surge propelled him at top speed. His heart pounded so hard he imagined he actually heard rather than just felt it. He pushed himself faster and faster. He had to reach her before she could get away. His shoes dug into the neatly manicured lawn. It was going to be very close.

Ten

Paige saw the gates start to swing shut. She pushed on the accelerator, forcing the car to go faster. She had to reach the end of the driveway before she was closed in, she had to get away. The tears streamed down her cheeks. The saltiness burned her eyes. She tried to wipe the tears away with one hand while keeping the other on the steering wheel. Her chest heaved and her body shuddered with each convulsive sob.

Through her clouded vision she saw the gates bang shut. She slammed on the brakes, skidding to a halt just inches from the blocked exit. She grasped the steering wheel in order to stop her hands from shaking, her grip so tight her knuckles turned white. She allowed her head to fall forward, coming to rest against her hands, then she sobbed uncontrollably.

Bryce reached her car a few moments after she braked to a halt just inside the closed gate. He yanked open her door and grabbed her arm. She tried to wrestle her arm from his grasp, but to no avail. He pulled her from the seat, backed her up to the fender, then pressed his body against hers.

She balled up her fists and shoved against his chest. She had to get away. She had to find someplace safe and quiet so she could sort things out, but his weight kept her pressed against the side of the car. Her words were filled with anger and pain. "Let me go...I don't want to ever see you again." She shoved harder, trying desperately to push him away from her.

He managed to gasp out a few words as he fought to catch his breath. "We have to talk." He grabbed her wrists as she tried to strike his chest again, grasping them tightly in his firm grip. "Stop it, Paige! Listen to me!"

She turned tear-filled eyes toward him as her sobs convulsed through her body. "How could you?"

He tried to make his voice as soothing as possible. "Calm down. Take a couple of deep breaths." He loosened his grip on her wrists. When she didn't fight him, he released his grasp, then enfolded her in his embrace. She seemed to be calming down. "There appears to be a lot of confusion here, confusion that has to be straightened out without further delay." He nestled her head against his shoulder and held her until she had better control.

The trepidation ran rampant through his consciousness. He smoothed the loose tendrils of hair away from her damp cheek, then kissed her teary eyelids. He felt her body shudder, then she slipped her arms around his waist and held him tightly. They stood next to her car clinging to each other for several minutes. Her sobs had lessened, but the tears still trickled down her cheeks and soaked into his shirt as she took the comfort and strength he gave her.

If she was confused before, now she was really confused.

She didn't know what to think or what to do. Everything was wrong.

Her words came out haltingly. "How could everything have become so terrible so quickly? How could you do that? How could you put all those people out of work for the sake of more profit?"

She could not contain her inner turmoil any longer. She blurted out the angry words, her voice filled with hurt. "What happened between you and my father?" Then another reality forced its way back into her consciousness, one that caused her just as much distress. Her voice dropped to a whisper as she made her painful confession. "I...I haven't been honest with you. I never told you the truth about who I—"

"Paige, don't say anything else." He put his fingertips to her lips to silence her. "You need a few minutes to calm down and collect yourself. Let's go back to the house." He had to stop her words, they were beginning to come out in a stream-of-consciousness flow, showing just how distraught she had become. He scooped her trembling body up in his arms and carried her across the lawn toward the house.

He was beginning to understand the full impact of what had happened. She saw the results of the board meeting, but had no knowledge of the second meeting that followed. Her guilt-filled words made it clear that she had been agonizing over what she thought was her deception in not telling him who she was.

What had shocked him the most were her words about his connection with her father's suicide. It was painfully obvious that she knew nothing about what Stanley Franklin had done, nothing of the circumstances that had led to his taking his own life rather than face public humiliation and legal prosecution. They definitely had lots to talk about, a great deal to straighten out. But would the information he was about to reveal put an end to what he hoped would be a permanent relationship? Would she accept what he had to offer?

Her body continued to tremble and the tears continued to slide down her cheeks even though the sobs had stopped. He carried her upstairs to his bedroom and placed her on the bed just as he had done the first time they made love. He pulled a quilt across the bed to cover her. He sat next to her, tucking the quilt tightly around her shoulders. He wiped the tears from her face, kissed her tenderly on the cheek, then held her in his embrace. He gently stroked her hair as he rocked her in his arms.

She felt so safe and protected in his embrace. The inner turmoil began to subside and a feeling of calm settled over her. He continued to rock her gently in his arms. Paige closed her eyes and allowed her mind to drift on a soft cloud to some faraway place.

The emotional upheaval had been too much for her. She felt completely drained. No sooner had she closed her eyes than she lapsed into the escape of an exhausted sleep. She wanted only happy thoughts and dreams. She conjured up mental images of the two of them married, of the children she had always wanted, of the loving home they could share. Somehow Bryce would be able to explain the things that had happened, explain his connection with her father. He would make everything okay.

Three hours passed without Paige waking. Bryce sat on the edge of the bed studying her, watching her as she slept. Her glossy auburn hair spread out across the pillow and against the side of her face in tangled strands. She was everything his life needed in order to be complete. His thoughts drifted, once again, to a wife and family. Maybe only two children if she wanted a small family. He, personally, wanted a larger family. He knew he had stored up enough love for whatever size family she wanted and would still have several lifetimes worth of love left over. He leaned forward and carefully smoothed the loose tendrils of hair away from her face as she continued to sleep.

Bryce finally left the bedroom to gather the materials he would need when he told her exactly what had transpired with her father many months ago and then what had happened following the board meeting that afternoon. The information about her father would undoubtedly be painful for her, but it had to be brought out into the open. There could be no secrets between them, not anymore, especially not one this important. As much as he wanted to protect her from the hurt, he knew there was no other way. He returned and sat on the edge of the bed. A constantly reverberating nervous surge swept through his body as he watched her sleep. He finally moved to a chair next to the bed. He picked up a book he had started to read a few days earlier and tried to concentrate on it, but success seemed to elude him.

Paige slowly became aware of being awake. She lay quietly with her eyes closed, trying to collect her thoughts and focus on reality. She had been enveloped in the most wonderful dream. The two of them were married. Their family consisted of four children...a gray cloud drifted across her memory of the dream. Could he possibly love her as much as she loved him? Was he the type who would be willing to settle down into marriage? Would he want a large family? Would he want children at all?

The pangs of guilt again stabbed at her. He did not know she was Stanley Franklin's daughter. She should have told him a long time ago, before the first time they made love. Whatever relationship they had was built on her deception. She loved him, but that love had been built on lies. She turned over on her back and stretched. She would take care of that matter immediately. She opened her eyes and looked around the room.

As soon as she stirred, Bryce put down the book and quickly moved to the bed, seating himself next to her. She had been asleep almost four hours. He had not wanted to wake her, she needed the rest, but he was glad she had not slept any longer. "Are you feeling better? Can I get you anything? A drink of water?"

She offered a shy smile, feeling somewhat foolish about her histrionics. The expression on his face showed his deep concern. She didn't know how long she'd been sleeping, but it must have been more than just a few minutes. "Yes, a drink of water…please."

He leaned forward and brushed his lips against hers. "I'll be right back."

As soon as he left the room she climbed out of bed and went to the balcony. The night air was damp and cool, but it felt good against her skin. She would not waste any more time. As soon as he returned she would tell him everything, get it all out into the open. She turned around when she heard him come back into the room. He joined her on the balcony, handing her the glass of water.

"Bryce…there's something I have to tell you—"

"You don't need—"

"Please let my finish, don't say anything until I've said what I have to say." The expression on his face told her he was vacillating between speaking and letting her have her way. He finally put his arm around her shoulder and escorted her back inside the room. They sat on the edge of the bed with him quietly honoring her request.

She clasped and unclasped her hands. The nervous energy flitted around inside her stomach. Finally she looked up, capturing the intensity of his turquoise eyes. "I…I haven't been honest with you, at least not completely honest. When I first applied for this job it was...well..."

She looked down at her trembling hands as she paused to take a calming breath, then finally blurted out the words in one long, nonstop sentence. "I'm Stanley Franklin's daughter and my original intention in taking this job was to find proof that you were responsible for ruining my father and causing his suicide, then stealing his company, only as time passed and things moved along I quickly realized that you weren't that type of person at all." She felt the tears well in her eyes. The butterflies in her stomach had divided into two armies and were engaged in battle. She gulped in a lungful of air. "You were so open and honest with me. I didn't know what to make of it. I managed to shove the thoughts and questions from my mind."

She glanced away as she collected her thoughts and formulated her words. "When we become intimately involved I wanted to be honest with you, but didn't know how or where to begin. I convinced myself that it didn't matter if you knew, that it had nothing to do with our personal relationship. But now..." A sob caught in her throat and her body trembled.

She turned her tear-filled eyes on him. Her deep anguish filled her voice and surrounded her words. "It was *unanimous*, that means you voted in favor of getting rid of Franklin Industries."

She tried to choke back another sob as she frantically searched his face, desperately wanting to find some truth and comfort. "How could you do that? Put one hundred people out of work just to put an extra dollar into your pocket? Those people have families to support, they have financial obligations that need to be met. They need those jobs." She had to know. She needed some sort of answer, some word from him that would tell her things were not the way they appeared.

He saw the hurt and pain. It tugged at his insides, the feeling compounded by the knowledge that what he had to do would hurt her even more. He picked up the file folders he had placed on the nightstand and set them on the bed next to her.

He took her face in his hands and settled a loving kiss on her lips. "I've always known you were Stanley Franklin's daughter. I also knew, even before meeting you, that you were doing your best to investigate every facet of my life and business. I waited, hoping you'd tell me about it. I never knew why you were doing it until now."

Her eyes opened wide in shock and her voice was filled with the surprise his statement created. "You knew? The job...everything...it was all a setup? A sham?"

"The job was legitimate. I couldn't imagine what you wanted, what you were looking for. Then, when you didn't tell me who you were, I didn't know what to think. You see, my mistake was in assuming that you knew about your father's company, about what had happened. It wasn't until today that I realized you truly didn't know anything about your father and what he had done."

He saw her shock turn to confusion, he felt her pain. This was the most difficult task that had ever presented itself to him. He had to purposely hurt the person he loved the most. He wrapped her in his embrace, burying his face in her hair. He held her tight against his body, then a moment later kissed her behind the ear. "I'd give everything I own to keep you from being hurt any more than you already have been, but I don't know what else I can do."

He reached for the first of the two file folders and handed it to her. "I don't keep everything in the computer. Some things are for my eyes only. This is one of those things. It was my intention that no one would ever see this, but under the circumstances…"

She took the file from him. A hard lump of trepidation settled in the pit of her stomach. Her hands trembled as she opened the folder.

She immediately recognized some of the papers as being the originals of ones she had discovered partially burned in her father's fireplace. She sat staring at the contents of the folder without really reading any of the reports. A cold chill spread through her body as she closed her eyes to compose her anxiety. Bryce had said enough for her to know that the file contained proof of her father's wrongdoing. Maybe it would be better if she just closed the file and gave it back without reading the contents.

No, that would not do. She would always wonder what had happened. It would always be an unsettled element of her life. No matter what, she had to put the matter to rest once and for all. She opened her eyes and picked up the top sheet of paper.

Bryce watched her carefully. Every thought and emotion she experienced clearly showed on her face. He wanted desperately to enfold her in his embrace and make all her pain and hurt go away, but he knew he couldn't. She would never feel comfortable and settled until she had all the facts. They would never be able to put this behind them and get on with their lives until the matter was history.

She began to carefully read each and every one of the numerous pieces of paper. Sometimes her hand would tremble and the tears would well up in her eyes and threaten to flow down her cheeks. It was those times when he most wanted to comfort and protect her. He felt the agony each time she picked up a particularly damning piece of evidence, each time her hand shook or a sob caught in her throat.

She was only halfway through the file when he took it from her hands and set it aside. He pulled her into his arms and stroked her hair. His voice was loving as he attempted to soothe away her torment. "Maybe you shouldn't read any more. It only gets worse."

His strength flowed to her, bolstering the sinking feeling that had settled deep inside her. She knew she was close to being in overload. If it were not for the fact that she loved and trusted Bryce she would have wondered if the facts had been tampered with or if the information was an out-and-out lie. Never in her life would she have imagined that her father could be involved with the things that were now coming to light for her. So many things that had puzzled her—the late-night phone calls behind locked doors, the clandestine meetings in out-of-the-way places—now they all made sense.

"No, I have to see all of it. I can't put this behind me until I know everything that happened." She took the file from him and returned to her reading. Almost an hour passed before she had finished with the last document. She closed the file and laid it aside.

Paige sat on the edge of the bed. Her face was pale and drawn and her eyes reflected a hollow emptiness. The anguish she felt was clearly visible to Bryce. His voice was soft, his words full of his own anguish. "I'm sorry, Paige. I hadn't planned to ever show that file to anyone. I wanted so much to protect you from the truth, to allow your final memories of your father to be good ones, but I had no choice."

Her voice was small, almost that of a child. "I had no idea. I never knew."

"I know." He kissed her tenderly on the cheek. "I know." He twined his fingers in her silky hair. "What can I do to help you with this? Do you want to talk? Do you want to be left alone for a while? What can I do? What do you need?''

She slipped her arms around his waist and rested her head against his shoulder. He was so caring, so generous. She did not know what she wanted or needed. She knew she didn't want to talk about it, at least not yet. She did not want to be alone either. She looked up at him, her gaze meeting the loving look in his eyes. "Could you just hold me for a while? Let me try to digest everything I've just read and see if I can make any sense of it?''

"Of course." He nestled her body next to his, cradling her in his embrace. Bryce leaned back against the headboard of the bed taking her with him. He allowed his mind to drift back over the contents of the file.

He had been doing a routine check of the financial statements and the books in preparation to purchasing what he thought was a healthy company. When he stumbled across the first of the irregularities in Stanley Franklin's books, he insisted on a thorough audit performed by his own team of accountants. While that was taking place, he had Joe Thompkins start an in-depth investigation into Stanley Franklin's personal life.

Bryce was shocked and disturbed by what Joe found. When the auditors finished their job, the results fit in with the information Joe had uncovered. The two reports together necessitated the immediate halt of all negotiations.

He still did not understand how it was possible for one man to so totally destroy everything he had spent a lifetime creating and in the end also destroy himself. That was bad enough, but now Stanley Franklin's downfall had extended its emotional toll to Paige. Bryce could forgive the man his own weakness, but he could not forgive him for what it was now doing to his daughter.

Paige was having difficulty understanding everything. It

was not so much what had happened as it was why it happened. The man she had just read about was a complete stranger to her, not the loving father she remembered from her childhood. It had been an unsettling time for her when her parents divorced while she was still in high school. At the time of her own divorce she took her newly acquired insight and looked back at that period in her life.

Upon reflection she realized that her parents had done everything right in the way they handled her emotional reaction. They were very careful to make sure she felt safe and secure no matter which one of them she was with. Each took care to not make derogatory comments about the other in her presence. Her mother had subsequently remarried and moved to the East Coast where she died a few years ago. Her father had never remarried.

She could not reconcile the man she remembered with the one she had just read about—a man who had embezzled from his own company until it was bankrupt, a man who had altered the books to cover the theft and used the money to pay off heavy gambling debts.

The files also revealed that when he had drained the company of all its funds, he began to refinance the company's assets, pledging the same assets as collateral for several different loans. After he had gone through that money, he began to borrow from a local notorious loan shark. It was the loan shark who had been responsible for the late-night phone calls and meetings in out-of-the-way places. It was the loan shark who had threatened him with severe bodily harm if he did not pay what he owed.

That had apparently been the final blow. Her father's note now made sense, he truly believed there was no other way out of the hell he had created for himself. A multitude of emotions washed over her—hurt…betrayal…anger. She also felt lost. Only the warmth and protection of Bryce's embrace kept her from being totally devastated. Her body trembled as she snuggled in his arms. She wanted him to squeeze her so tightly that she would not be able to feel anything else.

"Paige, honey…can I do anything for you, get you anything?" He brushed his lips against her cheek.

"No…there's nothing to do. I'll probably never fully understand why my father did what he did, how he became so heavily involved in gambling to the point of being a compulsive gambler, why he dealt with loan sharks." A hard tremor shot through her body.

She heard his strong heartbeat as he cradled her head against his chest. She raised her head and looked into his face, into the loving concern that emanated from his eyes. "At least I finally know the truth now. I don't need to spend the rest of my life wondering what happened." A quavering sigh escaped her lips. "Thank you for sharing the information with me."

"I wish there had been some way that wouldn't have been so painful for you." He kissed her lovingly on the lips. "There's more. I have another file you need to see. You expressed concern for the future of the company and the jobs of the employees. This should answer your questions and calm your fears."

She read the contents of the second file, carefully looking at every piece of paper and document. A warm feeling settled inside her as she realized the full impact of what she was seeing. There was a market study made at the time of her father's death that dealt with the impact on the community if the company was to be liquidated for debt payment, what opportunities there would be for the employees who would be laid off to find other jobs.

The file contained a memo to Bryce, dated just two days after her father's death, stating that the board opposed the purchase of the company and a response from Bryce saying he didn't want to see the employees lose their jobs. There were several pages of notes about restructuring and ongoing financial losses. The last items were from a meeting earlier that day, a meeting that followed the two o'clock board meeting.

Bryce had, indeed, voted with the board to rid the corporation of Franklin Industries. The vote was only a formality. It had already been discussed and decided that Bryce would take the company out of the corporation and retain ownership personally. There was a radical restructuring plan that would turn the company around in three years so that it would be profitable once again. He had allowed for a minimum of lost jobs with provisions for those few employees who would be terminated to be offered jobs in Bryce's other companies. There was also a budget that was conspicuous in its lack of any form of salary for Bryce.

She closed the file and set it aside. The love she felt for him so completely filled her, surpassing the anger and betrayal she felt toward her father. What Bryce had done with her father's company was similar to the way he had quietly taken care of Antonio and his family when they were in danger of losing their restaurant. She searched the depths of his eyes, then placed her fingertips against his cheek. "That was a very generous thing you did for the employees. I…I'm sorry I accused you—"

"You were upset. I understand." He twined his fingers through her hair, then traced her jawline with his fingertip. "We have so much to talk about, plans to make for our future." He hesitated, not sure if it was an appropriate time to talk about it. She had been through so much already, he was not sure…should he give her more time? Should he press on as if nothing had happened? He wasn't at all sure.

She allowed her mind to drift as she dissociated herself from the emotional place inside her that refused to deal with things in a logical and sensible manner. She viewed the situation, assimilated this new information about her father and reached her conclusions.

Her words were spoken in a soft voice, but they were neither hesitant nor uncertain. "I love my father for the man he was, the man who related to my life. The man he became in his final years was a stranger to me. I'll probably never understand why he did it, what drove him to his own destruction." She knew she could not dwell on it, could not let it eat away at her. There was nothing she could do to change the past. She needed to let go of the hurt, anger and feelings of betrayal. "All I can do is keep my good memories of a warm and loving father and forgive this stranger for what he's done."

Bryce scooted down on the bed taking her with him until they were lying next to each other. He continued to cradle her protectively in his embrace. They stayed together quietly for a long time. He did not want to interfere with her thoughts and her privacy.

At least two hours passed before Paige finally sat up and looked around. She turned toward Bryce, rested her hand against his cheek and placed a soft kiss on his lips. "Thank you."

"For what?"

"For being you and being so wonderful." Her inner turmoil had calmed. She felt at peace with the knowledge he had provided her.

Bryce took a calming breath. Now was the time to tell her. Now was the time to put everything on the line, to expose his most vulnerable inner feelings.

"My entire life I've been searching for that one special woman who would fill all my expectations and every time

I'd be disappointed when that person didn't measure up to the impossibly high standards I had created. I'd about given up ever finding that mythical woman—'' he brushed his lips against hers ''—until now.''

Wild surges of anxiety shoved at him, but it was too late to turn back. He forced the words he had been so carefully guarding. ''I love you, Paige. I love you very much.'' He cradled her face in his hands and looked into the depths of her eyes. ''Is there any chance that we have a future together?''

Paige saw the uncertainty in his eyes, the anxious look that covered his handsome features. She heard his words and the joy filled every corner of her reality.

''Oh, Bryce…you have no idea how much I've wanted to hear you say that. I love you so much and I was afraid my love would never be returned. Do we have a future together? If I have anything to say about it we most certainly do.''

He had never experienced such complete and pure happiness as at that moment. He pulled her into his arms and hugged her body tightly against his. ''You have made me the happiest man on the face of this planet. Now, tell me…what kind of wedding do you want to have? A big one or a small one?''

Her voice quavered slightly, not with the turmoil of earlier but the awe and wonder that filled her at that moment. ''Wedding? You mean like getting married?'' Her voice was barely above a whisper as she held her breath. ''Bryce?''

''I love you, Paige. I know this is a lot all at once. I hadn't planned on dealing with the situation of your father at this time. The only thing I had on my mind for this evening was to tell you how much I love you and ask you to marry me so that we can share the rest of our lives together.''

''Married? You want to marry me?'' Both her voice and face held her obvious surprise and elation.

He chuckled at her apparent disbelief. ''I love you and you love me. I want us to be together for the rest of our lives and eternity beyond that. I can't answer for you but I know I wouldn't feel right about any type of committed relationship that did not include our being married.''

The tears of happiness streamed down her cheeks, replacing the earlier tears of despair. ''Yes! Yes, I'll marry you.'' She wrapped her arms around his neck, the joy totally filling her until it threatened to burst the boundaries that barely contained it.

''Well, then...'' He slowly unbuttoned her blouse and placed a tender kiss on her throat. ''Would this be a good time to discuss starting a family?''

*   *   *   *   *

presents

DYNASTIES: THE CONNELLYS

A brand-new miniseries about the Connellys of Chicago,
a wealthy, powerful American family tied by blood to the
royal family of the island kingdom of Altaria.
They're wealthy, powerful and rocked by
scandal, betrayal...and passion!

Look for a whole year of glamorous and
utterly romantic tales in 2002:

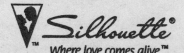

Silhouette®

Where love comes alive™

If you enjoyed what you just read,
then we've got an offer you can't resist!

Take 2 bestselling
love stories FREE!
Plus get a FREE surprise gift!

Clip this page and mail it to Silhouette Reader Service™

IN U.S.A.
3010 Walden Ave.
P.O. Box 1867
Buffalo, N.Y. 14240-1867

IN CANADA
P.O. Box 609
Fort Erie, Ontario
L2A 5X3

YES! Please send me 2 free Silhouette Desire® novels and my free surprise gift. After receiving them, if I don't wish to receive anymore, I can return the shipping statement marked cancel. If I don't cancel, I will receive 6 brand-new novels every month, before they're available in stores! In the U.S.A., bill me at the bargain price of $3.57 plus 25¢ shipping and handling per book and applicable sales tax, if any*. In Canada, bill me at the bargain price of $4.24 plus 25¢ shipping and handling per book and applicable taxes**. That's the complete price and a savings of at least 10% off the cover prices—what a great deal! I understand that accepting the 2 free books and gift places me under no obligation ever to buy any books. I can always return a shipment and cancel at any time. Even if I never buy another book from Silhouette, the 2 free books and gift are mine to keep forever.

225 SDN DNUP
326 SDN DNUQ

Name	(PLEASE PRINT)	
Address	Apt.#	
City	State/Prov.	Zip/Postal Code

* Terms and prices subject to change without notice. Sales tax applicable in N.Y.
** Canadian residents will be charged applicable provincial taxes and GST.
   All orders subject to approval. Offer limited to one per household and not valid to
   current Silhouette Desire® subscribers.
   ® are registered trademarks of Harlequin Books S.A., used under license.

DES02   ©1998 Harlequin Enterprises Limited

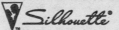

COMING NEXT MONTH

#1459 RIDE THE THUNDER—Lindsay McKenna
Morgan's Mercenaries: Ultimate Rescue
Lieutenant Nolan Galway didn't believe women belonged in the U.S.
Marines, but then a dangerous mission brought him and former marine pilot
Rhona McGregor together. Though he'd intended to ignore his beautiful copilot,
Nolan soon found himself wanting to surrender to the primitive hunger she
stirred in him....

#1460 THE SECRET BABY BOND—Cindy Gerard
Dynasties: The Connellys
Tara Connelly Paige was stunned when the husband she had thought dead
suddenly reappeared. Michael Paige was still devastatingly handsome, and
she was shaken by her desire for him—body and soul. He claimed he wanted to
be a real husband to her and a father to the son he hadn't known he had. But
could Tara learn to trust him again?

#1461 THE SHERIFF & THE AMNESIAC—Ryanne Corey
As soon as he'd seen her, Sheriff Tyler Cook had known Jenny Kyle was the
soul mate he'd searched for all his life. Her fiery beauty enchanted him, and
when an accident left her with amnesia, he brought her to his home. They soon
succumbed to the attraction smoldering between them, but Tyler wondered what
would happen once Jenny's memory returned....

#1462 PLAIN JANE MacALLISTER—Joan Elliott Pickart
The Baby Bet: The MacAllister Family
A trip home turned Mark Maxwell's life upside down, for he learned that
Emily MacAllister, the woman he'd always loved, had secretly borne him a
son. Hurt and angry, Mark nonetheless vowed to build a relationship with his
son. But his efforts brought him closer to Emily, and his passionate yearning for
her grew. Could they make peace and have their happily-ever-after?

#1463 EXPECTING BRAND'S BABY—Emilie Rose
Because of an inheritance clause, Toni Swenson had to have a baby. She
had a one-night stand with drop-dead-gorgeous cowboy Brand Lander, who
followed her home once he realized she might be carrying his child. When
Brand proposed a marriage of convenience, Toni accepted. And though their
marriage was supposed to be in-name-only, Brand's soul-stirring kisses soon had
Toni wanting the *real* thing....

#1464 THE TYCOON'S LADY—Katherine Garbera
The Bridal Bid
When lovely Angelica Leone fell into his lap at a bachelorette auction, wealthy
businessman Paul Sterling decided she would make the perfect corporate
girlfriend. They settled on a business arrangement of three dates. But Angelica
turned to flame in Paul's arms, and he found himself in danger—of losing his
heart!

SDCNM0802